I0598504

Abandoned But Not Lost

By Diane E. Izzard

Copyright © 2018 Diane E. Izzard

All Rights Reserved

This book is a work of fiction. References to real people, events, establishments, organizations, or locales are intended only to provide a sense of authenticity and are used fictitiously. Names, characters, incidents and dialogue are drawn from the author's imagination and not to be construed as real. Any resemblance to actual events or locales or persons, living or dead, is entirely coincidental.

Cover image used under license from shutterstock.com

ISBN: 978-0-9970065-4-4

Dedication

In loving memory of Morgan and Bear, my two German Shepherds
who brought me much joy during the twenty four years I was
blessed to have them in my life.

Acknowledgements

Many thanks to my family and friends for their loving support and constant encouragement.

Special thanks to Debbie Eye who always does an excellent job of catching all my errors and providing me with valuable input as my editor.

Much appreciation to Cheryl Clady for checking my proof and providing meaningful feedback. Your input was much appreciated.

Blessed are the peacemakers; for they shall be called the children of God.

St. Matthew 5:9

Chapter 1

Jo walked into Burt's Garage with the new carburetor he had requested in her hand. "Hey Burt, you back there?" Jo yelled, standing by the register.

"Come on in. I'm knee deep in grease," Burt shouted back.

"What are you working on today?"

"Miss Milly's old Cadillac is missing again. I'm just changing out the plugs, trying to get a few more miles out of it for her."

"I brought the new carburetor you ordered." Jo delivers parts for her father, who owns an automotive parts business in town.

"Thanks. Just set it on the counter for me."

"Who owns that beautifully restored 1959 cherry red Chevy truck out front?"

"I wish I knew. I got a call last night from the sheriff to have it towed. Charlie said it appeared to have been abandoned on Old Mill Pond Road." Burt wiped the grease from his hands and followed Jo outside.

Jo eyed the gorgeous silver rims and pristine cherry red paint. She opened the driver's side door to admire the interior. That's when she stopped in her tracks. A very large, tan and black German Shepherd stared back at her. "Nice doggy."

"I forgot to mention when I towed the truck here last night I heard a dog bark. I opened the door and found that beauty inside. He won't leave the truck, though. I've tried everything."

"You won't bite me, will you?" Jo asked cautiously as she held her hand out for him to sniff. "Good boy. What's your story?" She patted his smooth, silky, tan and black coat and looked into his deep brown eyes.

"He must be hungry. Have you tried giving him some food?"

"Yes, I gave him half of my baloney sandwich, but he wasn't interested."

"Let me try. I have a hamburger that I just picked up from the diner for lunch. If he can resist that, then there is something seriously wrong with him." Jo retrieved her take out order and removed the hamburger from the wrapper. "Here you go, boy." She took the patty out of the bun and broke it into small pieces into the palm of her hand.

The dog started to drool.

Jo held her hand up to his mouth. He gently ate the pieces from her hand. "Good boy!" Jo said as she patted him on the head. "Do you have a bowl I can use for water?"

Burt retrieved an empty whipped topping container he used to hold his bolts and washers when working on cars. He cleaned the container with soap to remove any grease, then filled it to the brim with water. "Here, see if you can get him to drink out of this."

Jo took the bowl and held it up to the dog's level. He sniffed it and then eagerly lapped up the water. "You said the truck was found abandoned?"

"Yeah, Charlie was doing his patrol yesterday and noticed the truck parked on the side of the road. He checked the license plate number in the system. There were no warrants out for the vehicle. He thought the owner must have left it after it broke down and would return later in the day to pick it up. When the truck was still sitting there after dark, he called me for a tow."

"You poor thing. You've been in this truck for two days now with no food or water." Jo continued to pat the dog. "He must belong to someone."

"The tag around his neck says his name is Moose."

"Does the tag have an address or phone number for Moose's owner?" Jo reached to look at the dog tag herself. The engraving was worn and the name was the only thing readable.

"I called Charlie this morning to ask if he had any luck locating the truck's owner. He said the name of the man listed on the truck's registration is deceased. The owner died a few months ago."

"Well, that's a start. A valuable truck like this must have been given to a family member or a close friend after he died."

"Who knows? All I do know is if the truck isn't claimed after thirty days the police will auction it off."

"What about Moose?"

"He seems to like you. If you can get him to leave the truck, maybe you can take him home."

"Come on, Moose." Jo slapped her leg, trying to get him to jump out of the truck.

Moose just gave her a sad look, then laid back down across the front seat to make it known he had no intention of leaving.

"That's all right, boy. You don't have to get out yet if you aren't ready. Maybe if you leave the door open he'll jump out on his own eventually."

"You can try that. I have to get back to fixen Miss Milly's car. You're welcome to stay with him for a while."

"No, I can't. Dad's probably wondering what's taking me so long. I need to get back to the store so I can help with customers."

"Why don't you stop back by after work and try again? I'll be here till six tonight."

"Will do." Jo patted Moose on top of his large head one last time. "I'll be back later this evening fella, to take you home," she said, hoping Moose understood. She returned to her black Dodge Ram she used as a delivery truck and drove away, feeling sad for the poor dog.

***

After work Jo stopped by the farm store. She glanced through the assortment of dog supplies and found a large breed twenty five pound bag of dry food. She also picked up some canned dog food in case Moose was not interested in the dry stuff. She

3

selected a big metal water bowl and food dish along with a box of treats, and a leash.

"That will be one hundred fifteen dollars and twenty three cents," the clerk said.

"Wow, I didn't realize how expensive it was to take care of a dog."

"Just wait till you have to take him to the vet," the clerk said.

Jo left the store with her bank account lighter but with her heart ready to help Moose however she could.

She arrived at Burt's Garage right at six. Burt was getting ready to close the shop for the night. She slowly walked up to the showroom's perfect Chevy truck that Moose had made his home. "Moose, are you still in there?" Jo asked cautiously as she peered through the open window. Moose lifted his large head and slowly wagged his tail at the sound of Jo's voice.

"Remember me? I'm the one that gave you that tasty burger for lunch." She reached inside the window and patted Moose on the head. "Are you hungry for some more food?" Jo asked tenderly.

Jo had placed some of the dry dog food in her jacket pocket. She opened the truck door. "I know you must be starved." She placed a few pieces of the dry dog food in her hand. "Here, I have something for you," Jo said has she held her hand up to Moose's nose.

He smelled the food without much enthusiasm. "Come on boy, try a little for me."

As if he understood, Moose took a little of the food from her hand and slowly ate it. Then he finished what was in her hand.

"Good boy!" Jo praised Moose. She reached back in her pocket and pulled out another handful of food. Moose gobbled it up this time. Jo filled the water bowl and placed in on the seat in front of Moose. He smelled the water then drank eagerly until the bowl was empty.

"I know you must have to pee. How about you jump down out of that truck?" Jo held the truck door open widely, hoping to encourage Moose to hop out.

He laid on the seat looking sadly around outside. Jo decided if Moose wasn't going to leave, then she would sit in the truck with him. Moose's large body took up most of the front seat. Jo managed to scoot in under Moose's enormous head. She started caressing his head, with each stroke talking calmly to him. "I know you are sad and want your owner back. We're never going to find him or her, though, if you don't leave this truck. I have a small house with a large back yard. If you would come with me, I'll take good care of you until we find your owner. What do you think about that?" Jo hooked the leash to Moose's collar. She slowly eased out of the truck, holding tightly to the leash. She held out one of the treats she had bought. "Come on, boy. I know you can do it!"

To her surprise, Moose responded. He jumped down from the seat onto the ground. "Good boy!" She rewarded him with the treat. She led him to the nearest tree. Moose watered the tree for several minutes. With another treat in hand, she coaxed him to her old black 1998 Dodge Ram. She placed a treat on the passenger seat and Moose jumped in after it. She quickly closed the door before he could jump back out. She returned to the truck Moose had made home to retrieve his water bowl, and that's when she noticed something stuck behind the seat. She folded the seat forward so she could reach the object. She lifted a camouflage backpack from the floor. "This must belong to Moose's owner," she excitedly said to herself. She quickly unzipped it and rummaged through the contents for any identification. There were just a few clothes and essential bathroom products. She decided to take the backpack with her and perform a more thorough search when she arrived home. She locked the truck and returned to her Dodge Ram where Moose had his nose glued to the driver's side window, watching her every move.

"Scoot over and give me a little room," Jo said as she shoved Moose to the passenger side. She rolled the window just far enough down so Moose could stick his nose out. He enjoyed the smells as she drove home. She pulled into her dirt driveway and parked underneath the carport beside her house.

"Well, boy, what do you think of your new home?"

Moose looked through the windshield and perked up when he saw a squirrel run up the large oak tree in the back yard. She grabbed hold of his leash and opened the driver's side door. "How about we go check out the back yard?"

Moose jumped out of the truck. Words from the Dog Whisperer television show popped in Jo's head. You need to make sure your dog knows you're the leader of the pack. Also, you have to show your dog the boundaries. Jo tried to act dominant and led Moose around the perimeter of the back yard. She hoped he was smart enough not to run off when she removed the leash. Her property bordered a cattle farm. A barbed wire fence was the only thing keeping the cows off her property. The cows seemed to think the grass in her back yard tasted better than what was in their pasture. They were forever breaking through the fence. Moose didn't pay much attention to the cows and must not have considered them a threat. He did seem fixated on the large oak tree where the squirrel chatted away at him, though. He marked his new territory, stopping to leave his scent several times around the edge of the lot.

Once inside the house, Jo showed Moose the rooms where he would be allowed to occupy. "This is the kitchen where we'll eat. No jumping on the counters or table. This is our bedroom. You will sleep on the floor. Finally, this is the family room. There will be no jumping on the furniture. What do you think?"

Moose barked for the first time, to Jo's delight. She unclipped the leash from Moose's collar so he could walk freely throughout the house. She placed his food in the pantry and bowls on the kitchen floor. "How about we get a little more to eat?"

Moose barked again as Jo poured some dry food in his dish. This time he didn't hesitate and ate everything in the bowl in seconds. He lapped up another bowl of water. Jo looked through the sparse contents of the refrigerator. She wasn't much for grocery shopping or cooking. She removed a couple of hotdogs from the zip lock storage pouch. She zapped them in the microwave for a minute. Then she placed them in a bun and covered them with mustard and cole slaw. Moose watched patiently, lying by her feet as she ate. She quickly discovered that wherever she went, Moose followed. At bedtime, she laid an old blanket on the floor by her bed. "Here you go, boy. You can sleep here." She climbed into bed and rolled over on her side to find Moose's enormous head just inches from her face. He stared at her with his big, brown pleading eyes. She groaned in defeat. "All right, have it your way. Sleep wherever you want." With an effortless leap Moose jumped on the bed and laid his enormous head across her chest. She slowly stroked his silky coat until they both fell asleep.

***

The next morning Jo woke to the sound of her cell phone alarm going off. It was time to get ready for work. "Okay, boy! It's time to start another day. Do you need to go out before I get in the shower?"

Moose leaped off the bed and barked. She took that as a sign that meant yes. She threw on some sweats and clipped the leash to his collar. She didn't trust him enough yet to let him run free. Moose quickly did his business, then barked at the birds and squirrels scurrying around the back yard. "We don't have time to play this morning, but I promise to let you run around after work."

She led Moose back inside the house, then started the coffee maker before jumping in the shower. Moose followed her into the bathroom. "I know you want to stay close, but I need some privacy." She pushed Moose out of the entrance to the bathroom, then closed the door on his nose before he could get back in. She quickly showered, not sure what Moose may get into while she was getting ready. She draped a towel around her slender body and opened the bathroom door to find Moose laying on the floor in front of the door. "Have you been waiting for me this entire time? You are such a good boy!" She praised Moose while she slipped on jeans and a shirt with her Dad's automotive store logo of a red 1956 Ford F100 on the pocket. She placed her bronze hair in a ponytail to tame the many natural curls. She applied a little makeup even though her smooth complexion allowed her to easily go without. She was blessed to be blemish free and still too young to have any wrinkles to conceal.

"How about some food?" Moose barked with anticipation. Jo poured about two cups of dry dog food in his bowl and placed it on the floor. It was gone before Jo could fill his water dish. "Well, you are definitely making up for the lack of food the last two days." She opened a can of moist beef flavored dog food and dumped the entire contents it into his bowl. He inhaled it while she filled her travel mug with coffee. She stuffed a blueberry pop tart in her jacket pocket to eat when she got to work, and searched for her car keys. "Found them!" she rejoiced to Moose. One glance at the clock told her she was going to be late to work again if she didn't hurry. "Come on Moose, you're going with me today." She didn't have the heart to leave him alone.

Moose eagerly followed and jumped into her Dodge Ram as soon as she opened the door. Jo smiled at how obedient he was. It was almost as if he could read her mind.

Jo arrived at work within ten minutes and entered her father's store with Moose by her side. "Who do we have here?" Jo's Dad asked.

"Dad, I'd like you to meet Moose. He was abandoned on Old Mill Pond Road. Burt found him in a gorgeous 1959 Chevy truck he towed. I'm looking after him until his owner can be found. I hope you don't mind if he stays with me while I work."

"Not at all. I don't think he'll scare off any customers. Most of them are dog lovers anyway and have dogs of their own. I have a few deliveries waiting for you this morning."

Jo took the parts and order receipts. Moose followed her back to her truck and jumped in without any hesitation. She placed the parts on the floor, cracked the window for Moose to enjoy the cool morning air, and headed to their first stop.

"You stay here. I'll only be a minute," Jo told Moose as she stepped out of the truck. Moose started barking wildly at being left behind. She quickly delivered the part and returned to the truck.

"It's okay, boy," she consoled Moose. "I'm right here. You obviously don't like it when I'm out of sight. I won't leave you again."

The next stop she let Moose follow her into the garage to deliver the part. He stayed glued to her right side.

"Who is your new helper?" Mr. Sikes, the shop owner, asked.

"This is Moose. I'm watching after him until we find his owner. If you hear of anyone that has lost their Shepherd send them my way."

"He sure is a beauty. I can't believe anyone would let him run off."

"Yeah, I know what you mean. It's hard for me to believe also. Have a good day Mr. Sikes!" Jo yelled as she left his business.

"How about we stop and talk to Sheriff Charlie on our way back to work? Maybe he has some news on your owner."

Charlie could always be found at the diner this time of morning with a cup of coffee and donut in hand. "Hey Charlie! Catching any speeders this morning?"

"Pretty quiet other than Miss Cathy complaining about her neighbor's goats eating her begonias." There wasn't much crime in the small town of Wheeler. The most excitement this town ever saw was when Mr. Folkston forgot to close his cattle gate and there were fifty cows running loose down Main Street. It took most of the day to round them up and get them back inside the fenced pasture.

"I was wondering if you've had any luck finding the owner of the truck that was abandoned."

"That must be the German Shepherd Burt found inside." Moose stood obediently close to Jo's side.

"Yes, I can't believe someone would have willingly left such a special dog inside. Did you see anything suspicious in the area where the truck was left that would indicate someone may have disappeared unwillingly?"

"You know, I wasn't really looking for anything illegal. At the time, I figured the old truck had just broke down, and the owner just left it by the side of the road to retrieve at a later date. It was dark and I didn't realize the dog was laying down inside. I'll drive back out there today and take a look. I'll also talk to the neighbors and see if they saw anyone needing assistance."

"That would be great! While you do that, could you give me the name on the truck registration and maybe I can find Moose's owner that way?"

"Like I told Burt, Clark Davis died a few months ago. It was registered in Lorly County, down south."

"That's a couple hours away. Do you think it's possible that someone may have stolen the truck and ditched it here before they got caught?"

"I checked and the truck was not reported stolen, so that's unlikely. Plus, why would someone steal a truck and then leave their dog inside?"

"Yeah, I guess you're right. Can you do a little digging to find out if Mr. Davis had any relatives? They might know who the truck was given to after he died."

"When I talked to the Sheriff at the Lorly police station, he said Mr. Davis owned a pizza parlor. He died of a heart attack a few months ago. He didn't offer any more information."

"Well, that's a start. I'll search for a phone number to the pizza parlor Mr. Davis owned. If it's still in operation, maybe someone still working there knows who Mr. Davis gave his truck to."

"If you find anything that might indicate something illegal occurred, let me know immediately. I don't want you getting yourself in trouble. Your Dad would never forgive me if anything happened to you."

"Don't worry, Charlie. I'm just trying to return Moose to his owner. I'll be careful."

***

As soon as Jo returned to the auto parts store, she started searching for all the pizza parlors located in Lorly. In between customers, she wrote down the eight phone numbers listed in the white pages. That night she called each one, asking if a Clark Davis used to own the business. Finally, at the sixth pizza parlor, she talked to someone who knew Clark Davis.

"I actually purchased the business from a representative of Clark Davis. When I saw the For Sale sign in the window, I contacted the number listed and made arrangements to buy the business. Clark Davis's trustee actually handled the sale of the property."

"Did you know Mr. Davis personally?" Jo asked.

"No, I'm sorry. I never met the man."

"By any chance, did you hire any of the previous employees that worked for Mr. Davis?"

"No, I don't think so. It was closed for about two months before I was able to reopen it as an Italian restaurant. This is not the type of business where employees stay for any length of time."

"Can you give me the name of Mr. Davis's trustee that handled the sale?"

"Sure, I think I still have his number in my wallet. Hang on. Here it is. His name is Daniel Alexander."

"Thanks for your help. Good luck with your new business." Jo hung up the phone and immediately called the number she was given. An answering machine picked up indicating that the business was closed. She would have to try again in the morning.

Moose sat on the floor by her foot, patiently waiting for her to get off the phone. "I bet you're hungry aren't you, and ready to go out and get some exercise?"

Moose spoke up by barking at the mention of food. He waited patiently by his food dish until Jo retrieved his bag. She placed a large scoop of the food in his bowl. Within seconds it was gone.

"Slow down, boy, and at least taste what you're eating."

Moose washed down his food, lapping up his bowl of water. The water sloshed all over the floor as he licked up every drop until the bowl was dry. Jo watched in amazement at how he made sure his food dish was licked clean to make sure he didn't miss a crumb.

After supper she sat in the back yard with Moose and watched while he played. He ran around the perimeter of the yard, glad to be running freely. He patrolled the yard to make sure it stayed free of any critters that might threaten his domain. The squirrels quickly learned to keep an eye out for Moose and just how high he could jump. They would scurry just far enough up the tree so he couldn't reach them. They teased him incessantly with their chatter. This noise only made Moose run around the base of the tree barking nonstop.

"Boy, do you want to play ball?" Jo asked in hopes of breaking his fixation on the squirrels. She threw an old tennis ball as far as she could across the back yard. Moose raced after it, tossed the ball in the air, then caught it in his mouth, before racing back to Jo and dropping the ball at her feet.

This game went on until Moose was finally exhausted. He returned to Jo's side but kept the ball in his mouth, squishing it between his jaws. He collapsed by her feet. He eventually dropped the ball, panting profusely to cool down. The sun was dipping below the horizon and the temperature was dropping quickly.

"I don't know about you, but I'm getting cold. Are you ready to go inside and call it a night?"

Moose barked his response. Jo stood up and Moose quickly followed. On the way to wash up, Jo spotted the backpack on the sofa where she had thrown it the night before. She lifted the velcro pockets on the side and removed the contents. There was a comb, toothbrush, toothpaste, razor, socks, a pad of paper, and an ink-pen. She unzipped the center of the backpack. She pulled out a pair of cargo shorts, jeans, three black t-shirts, sweats, two flannel shirts, five pairs of brief underwear with a camouflage design, and a faded blue jean jacket. Moose laid his head on the sofa and sadly watched as Jo sorted through his owner's belongings. There was no wallet or identification of any kind.

"Moose, your owner sure is organized and travels light." Feeling a little uneasy about rummaging through someone else's belongings, she placed the contents back inside the pack as she had found them.

Jo decided there was nothing more she could do tonight to find Moose's owner. She shared a bowl of vanilla ice cream covered in chocolate syrup with Moose while she contemplated what Daniel Alexander might share with her in the morning. Too tired to think any more, she got ready for bed. She climbed beneath the covers and Moose immediately followed with a thud. He circled until he was finally satisfied, then plopped down with a sigh and rested his head across Jo's chest.

Jo lay awake stroking Moose's smooth coat, wondering about his story. She tried not to let herself become attached to Moose, knowing he would eventually be returned to his owner. But it was hard not to. He had a special soul that seemed to sense her needs and responded accordingly. He was the best boyfriend she'd ever had. Jo hadn't had much luck in the guy department. She was an intelligent, strong-willed woman that seemed to threaten the men she met. When they discovered they couldn't control her, they were quickly out of her life. Jo was looking for someone that was adventurous, funny, and enjoyed a challenge, but surely not someone that just went through life not expecting much out of it. As she drifted off to sleep, she imagined the type of person Moose's owner must be, muscular, tall, with dark compassionate eyes.

Chapter 2

The next morning, Jo arrived at work early so she could spend some time trying to reach Daniel Alexander before making her deliveries. She dialed the number she was given once again, hoping to speak to a person and not a machine.

Jo was rewarded when a woman answered the phone.

"Alexander Attorney at Law, can I help you?"

"Yes, could I speak to Mr. Alexander?"

"I'm sorry, he's currently with a client. Would you like to leave a message or set up an appointment?"

"I need to ask him about Clark Davis. I was told Mr. Alexander handled his estate. It's urgent that I talk with him. Could you ask him to call me back at this number?"

"His schedule is pretty busy this morning, but he might have time this afternoon."

"That would be great," Jo said as she ended the call.

Jo hurriedly made her morning deliveries. She stayed busy and jumped at the phone every time it rang. Finally at around 2 o'clock Mr. Alexander returned her phone call.

"Mr. Alexander, thank you so much for taking the time to talk with me. Clark Davis's truck was found abandoned in Wheeler this week. I'm hoping you might be able to tell me who received his belongings after his death."

"Mr. Davis didn't have any living family. He donated most of his estate to charity."

"Do you remember who he gave his '59 Chevy pickup to?"

"Oh yes. I do remember that truck. It took him years to restore it and then he rarely drove it. There was a young man that worked at his pizza parlor that he became quite fond of. He treated him like a son. Just before his death he updated his will to make sure the truck was given to him."

"Can you give me the man's name?"

"I'm afraid that's privileged information."

"I think the man's life might be in jeopardy. Surely under special circumstances you could make an exception and divulge that information."

"What makes you think this person is in trouble?"

"Mr. Davis's Chevy truck was found abandoned with a German Shepherd named Moose inside. I don't know if you own a dog, Mr. Alexander, but all the dogs I ever owned were part of our family. There is no way I would have left Moose inside that truck unless I felt he would be safer. This dog has been well cared for. I can't believe his owner would have left him unless that was the only way to protect him."

Mr. Alexander did not immediately respond, while he tried to figure out how to best handle the situation. "I guess there would be no harm in giving you the name of an employee that used to work for Clark Davis."

Jo understood that Mr. Alexander was protecting himself legally. "Yes, all I need is the employee's name. It has nothing to do with Mr. Davis's will."

"A man by the name of Wyatt Deckster used to work as a cook for Clark Davis."

"You wouldn't happen to have a home address or phone number for Mr. Deckster, would you?"

"Let me check my records. I might have a phone number where I contacted him. Yes, here it is. Unfortunately, I don't think this will help you. It's the business phone number for the pizza parlor. He lived in a small room above the business at the time. Since then the business has been sold, so I'm sure he doesn't live there any more."

"Sorry to hear that. I'll see if I can find any information online. Thank you so much for your time and help."

Jo was ecstatic that she now had a name. She immediately got on the computer to see what popped up when she typed in Wyatt Deckster. Disappointment greeted her. There were no matches that tied the name to the Lorly area, or that looked promising. There wasn't even a phone number listed in the white pages. Her mood quickly sank to dismal at the realization that she was no closer to finding Moose's owner.

On the way home she spotted Charlie's cruiser parked outside the diner. She found Charlie inside enjoying the meatloaf and gravy special of the day.

"Hey there, young lady. Surprised to see you again so soon."

"I discovered a guy by the name of Wyatt Deckster was given Mr. Davis's truck after he passed away."

"Is that so?"

"Did you have a chance to talk to anyone on Old Mill Pond Road today to see if they saw anyone needing assistance?"

"Yes, I interviewed a few people, but no one I spoke with saw anyone needing help."

"Did you examine the area where the truck was found to see if anything looked out of the ordinary?"

"I stopped along the side of the road, but didn't notice anything that would indicate there was a struggle or crime committed."

"He couldn't have vanished into thin air."

"When I get back to the station, I'll see what information I can find on Wyatt Deckster in the system. That's about all I can do."

Jo left not satisfied. She had a bad feeling that something terrible had happened to Wyatt. She decided to drive down Old Mill Pond Road herself before it got dark. It was just a few miles outside of town. She turned down the narrow, roughly paved, winding road. There was not another car in sight. She drove slowly, looking on both sides of the road. Nothing stood out to her. Then Moose started barking wildly. "What is it, boy?" She stopped her truck and pulled over. She opened the truck door to take a closer look. Moose sprang from the truck and took off running into the woods.

Jo yelled, "Moose, stop!" He ignored her command.

Jo had no choice but to run after him. She sprinted through the woods, narrowly missing a low tree limb from ramming her in the head. She ran until her lungs were about to explode. I really need to start working out, she thought to herself. She stopped to catch her breath. Moose was nowhere in sight. She tried calling to him. "Moose, come boy. Where are you?"

She heard him bark in the distance. She rushed toward the sound. The barking became more persistent. She approached the large pond the road was named after, and saw Moose standing in the high grass near the bank. He was barking at something in the grass. She just hoped it wasn't a rattlesnake. She cautiously approached. "What is it, boy?" She peered in front of Moose at a motionless body lying facedown in the grass. "Moose, is this your owner?" She carefully turned the body over, trying not to cause any additional harm. His face was covered in dirt and what appeared to be bug bites. She looked for any signs of life. The body was very pale. There was dried blood caked in his hair above his forehead and on the grass. She felt for a pulse at the side of his neck. She was shocked when she felt a thump against her finger.

"He's still alive Moose! We've got to get him some help." She pulled out her cell phone. She barely had one bar. She had Charlie's number in her contact list and pressed call.

"Charlie, this is Jo. I think I found Wyatt Deckster. He needs an ambulance."

"You're breaking up, Jo. Who did you find?"

"Just get an ambulance to Old Mill Pond Road. Come to the pond!" Jo yelled as the call dropped. She hoped Charlie understood. The temperature was starting to drop as the sun set. She removed her suede jacket and used it to cover Wyatt's chest. Moose seemed to sense that she was trying to keep him warm. He laid his massive body against Wyatt's torso.

"Hang in there, Wyatt! Help is on the way." Jo hoped he could hear her.

The sound of sirens could be heard in the distance. When they grew loud and stopped, Jo yelled, "Over here!" She continued yelling until Charlie and the EMTs came into sight. Jo stepped out of the way and held onto Moose as they started prepping Wyatt for transport.

"It's all right, boy. They'll take good care of him. You'll see him again soon." Jo hugged Moose tightly around the neck as he tried to pull away from her. They watched as Wyatt was loaded into the back of the ambulance and as it drove away.

***

Jo arrived at the hospital not long after the ambulance. She parked and rushed inside the emergency room with Moose by her side.

"Hey! That dog can't be in here," someone yelled from behind the desk.

Jo thought fast. "He's a therapy dog and his owner, Wyatt Deckster, was just brought in," she blurted out. "I know he'll want to see Moose as soon as he's conscious." She hoped the lady behind the desk would sympathize with her.

The woman hesitated then said, "I guess it wouldn't hurt for you stay in the waiting area with the dog."

"Thank you so much." Jo sat down in one of the lightly padded vinyl covered chairs that lined the wall. Moose sat beside her, leaning the full weight of his body against her knee. Jo hugged Moose and reassured him, "You'll see him again soon. You're such a good boy!" She stroked his head until exhaustion set in. Moose slid down to the floor beside her, resting his tired head on top of her feet.

Evening turned into night and there was still no word on Wyatt's condition. Jo drifted off to sleep, resting the back of her head against the wall. She felt a tap on her arm. She slowly opened her eyes and focused on the nurse standing above her. It was Judy, a friend of Jo's who worked the night shift.

"Oh, hey Judy. I must've fallen asleep," Jo said as she yawned. "Can you find out how Wyatt Deckster is doing for me?"

"I ran into Charlie in the hall and he filled me in on what happened. I checked with his nurse and Wyatt is holding his own but has not regained consciousness. It looks like someone tried to put a bullet through his head. The bullet was stopped by a metal plate that had been put in place after a previous head injury. What do you know about this guy?"

"Unfortunately, I know almost nothing about him other than he traveled from Lorly to here and abandoned his truck on Old Mill Pond Road three days ago."

"Doctors are keeping a close eye on him. Why don't you go home and get some rest? If there is any change in his condition, I'll give you a call."

"Thanks Judy. I would appreciate that." Jo had to drag Moose back to her truck. He wanted to stay near Wyatt. "I promise I'll bring you back in the morning," Jo told Moose as she coaxed him through the parking lot.

After only a few hours of restless sleep, Jo got up and fixed herself a strong cup of coffee to get her brain working. After feeding Moose she drove to work. She made herself comfortable behind the counter and hoped business would be slow and she wouldn't have to move. She tried to focus on helping the customers while Moose laid across her feet while he slept. That way if she moved, he would know. She had just returned from the back store room to get a part for a customer.

"Here you go, Mr. Harper," Jo said as she handed him the part.

"Jo, what is this?" Mr. Harper asked.

Jo looked down at the carburetor in his hand.

"I needed a distributor cap, not a carburetor," he said as he handed the part back to Jo.

"I'm sorry Mr. Harper. I don't know where my head is today." Jo retrieved the correct part and rang up his purchase. She processed his charge card and handed him the receipt.

As soon as he left the store, Jo's Dad spoke up, "Why don't you go to the hospital and see how Moose's owner is doing? I can handle things here for the rest of the day."

"Really? That would be great, Dad!" She leaned over and kissed him on the cheek. "Come on Moose. Let's go visit Wyatt." Moose jumped up and ran to the door, waiting for Jo to catch up. He waited patiently for her to open the passenger door so he could leap inside.

After explaining Moose was a therapy dog once again to the another person behind the desk, Jo and Moose were allowed to enter the hospital and were provided Wyatt's room number. Jo quietly entered ICU and located Wyatt's room. He was hooked up to a few tubes and his head was bandaged, but surprisingly he looked like he was resting comfortably. He was breathing on his own and his skin color had turned from pale white to tan. Jo made herself comfortable in a chair by the bed, and Moose rested his large head on Wyatt's hand lying at the edge of the bed. She wasn't sure what to say or do. Before she could figure it out, Wyatt started to stir. Moose became alert and barked. Wyatt started thrashing around and Jo was afraid he might hurt himself. She yelled for a nurse.

Chapter 3

They were guided by the stars on this moonless night. Their mission was to rescue a soldier that had been captured. They had been through strenuous training and followed their instinct without having to think. Hiding in the shadows, they grew closer to the compound. It was eerily quiet. There was no one standing guard. It couldn't be this easy, Wyatt thought. He remained alert, fearful they might be ambushed. He approached a stone building with his AK47 lifted, ready to fire at the first sign of the enemy. Wyatt approached the entrance and listened. There was silence. He pressed forward and watched his best friend Roy enter the building in front of him. A loud explosion broke the silence. All went dark.

The pain was excruciating. Wyatt moaned and could hear voices speaking to him.

"Stop! You're going to hurt yourself," Jo said as she grabbed his arm to keep him from ripping out the IV.

A nurse came rushing in and helped restrain him.

Wyatt stopped resisting when he heard a familiar bark. "Moose, is that you?" he tried to say out load, but no words came out. He struggled to open his eyes, but it was so bright. The light sent piercing pain through his head.

"Wyatt, you're in the hospital. Moose is here with you," Jo said as she tried to get him to calm down.

The woman's voice sounded familiar to him. He slowly opened his eyes and tried to focus. A pretty brunette, with untamed curly hair, and eyes the color of gingerbread was holding his arm down. Then he saw Moose, and smiled.

Jo and the nurse released his arms. The nurse repeated, "You're in the hospital and have had an accident."

Jo spoke up, "My name is Jo. I've been watching Moose for you."

Wyatt used what little strength he had to slowly stroke Moose's massive head that laid by his hand on top of the covers.

The doctor walked in and said, "Glad to see you are awake. How are you feeling, Mr. Deckster?"

He tried to speak again and managed to whisper, "Like a freight train ran over me."

"Good, that means you're on the road to recovery. I can give you a little medicine to help ease the pain, but as you probably are already aware, with a head injury we try to limit the amount of pain meds so the patient doesn't drift back into a coma."

Wyatt slowly lifted his hand to touch the bandage wrapped around his head, as he tried to remember what had happened.

Jo spoke up, "Moose helped me find you off Old Mill Pond Road after someone put a bullet in your head. Do you remember anything?"

Wyatt thought for a while before speaking. "What city am I in?"

"Wheeler. I think you drove here from Lorly in your truck. Do you remember working for a Clark Davis at his pizza parlor?"

Wyatt strained to remember. "Mr. Davis died, didn't he?"

"Yes, I'm afraid so."

"He was a good man." Wyatt's speech started to slur.

The doctor turned on a penlight and flashed it in Wyatt's eyes to check his responsiveness. "You're a very lucky man. If Jo hadn't found you when she did, you may not have survived. What you need now is rest. You have a traumatic brain injury and shouldn't try pushing yourself too much just yet. Your memory may be a little foggy, but it should come back in a few days."

The nurse gave him some medicine to help him rest. Wyatt's eyes became very heavy. No matter how hard he tried, he couldn't keep them open.

The doctor turned to Jo. "He'll be in and out of consciousness for a few days. If you would like, why don't you come back in the morning?"

"Thanks, doctor," Jo said. Moose reluctantly left with Jo. On the way to her truck, she bumped into Charlie.

"How is Wyatt doing?" Charlie asked.

"Good news! He woke up, but the bad news is he doesn't seem to remember what happened to him. The doctor doesn't want him to overdo it and asked me to leave. Were you able to uncover any additional information about him?"

23

"As a matter of fact I did. He was a member of Special Forces in the Army for eight years. He was injured in Afghanistan about a year ago and was forced to leave the service."

"That might explain what nurse Judy told me. She said he had a metal plate in his head. That is what stopped the bullet from doing more damage."

"I wasn't able to find a driver's license or any other information about where he has been living since he left the military."

"Maybe he was at a medical facility having physical therapy after his injury."

"That's possible. You said he worked at a pizza place in Lorly, right?"

"Yes, that's what Mr. Alexander, Clark Davis's attorney, told me. Wyatt also confirmed that info to me just now when I told him where he came from. I was hoping it might bring back his memory of what happened to him."

"I'm going to see if the doctor will let me talk to him while he is still awake."

"You may be too late. Wyatt was administered some medicine and was falling back to sleep when I left."

"Then I guess I'll have to wait until he's conscious again."

"I'm headed home. Let me know if Wyatt is able to remember what happened to him. I would hate to think there's a murderer running loose in our county," Jo said.

Jo stopped by The Burger Hut on the way home. Their burgers and home fries are the best in the state. After picking up her order at the take out window, she drove home. Jo felt something moist seep through her jeans and looked over at Moose. Drool was dripping from Moose's mouth onto her leg. The tantalizing smell of the burgers had him salivating uncontrollably.

"Don't worry, I didn't forget about you! I bought you a hamburger, also." Jo rubbed the top of Moose's head.

After supper, Moose quickly ran around the back yard to clear it of any trespassers before returning inside to stay close to Jo. Jo made herself comfortable on the sofa, propping her head up with a pillow, and Moose scooted in beside her. She channel surfed until she stopped on a car restoration show on the television. With her stomach full, it was only a few minutes before she fell fast asleep on the sofa with Moose snoring quietly beside her.

Chapter 4

Jo woke with a start at the sound of Moose barking loudly. "All right buddy, I'm awake. What is it?" Jo looked around the room and noticed the family room window was open. She heard the sound of a vehicle engine starting outside. She quickly jumped off the sofa and glanced out the window just in time to see the tail lights of a dark colored SUV racing away. With the yellow glow coming from the streetlight out front of her home, she could barely make out that is was a Jeep Cherokee. She was now fully awake. She closed the window and securely locked it. She hurriedly looked around the house to see if anything was missing. She convinced herself there was no way anyone would come inside with Moose standing guard. Moose's large ears were always on alert, even when he was asleep.

She returned to the sofa and embraced Moose. "You are such a good boy. You scared away whoever was trying to get inside." She kissed Moose on top of the head.

"Who the heck would want to break into my place? It's not like I have anything of value worth stealing," she told Moose.

She went to bed but laid awake stroking Moose's silky coat, unable to sleep. She thought about Wyatt and wondered what his story could possibly be. The horrible things he must have experienced in Afghanistan. Being seriously injured twice now, once protecting our country and then here with someone trying to kill him. Where is his family? Surely he has someone in his life that must be worried about him. Why didn't they contact authorities to file a missing person's report? So many questions were running through her head. She finally gave up getting any more sleep and dragged herself out of bed at six. She wanted to visit Wyatt before she went to work to see if he could fill in any of the missing pieces to his life.

She opened the back door to let Moose run around outside to get his morning exercise. She watched Moose through the kitchen window as he cleared the yard of squirrels and scared away the birds chirping in the trees. She started a pot of strong coffee. Before the coffee could finish dripping, she heard Moose scratch at the door to let her know he was ready to come in. She opened the door and Moose came barreling inside. "Well, you didn't waste any time this morning. Do you want some breakfast?"

Jo poured some beef flavored dog food in his dish and Moose gobbled it down in thirty-seconds flat. Water sloshed all over the floor as he hurriedly drank from his bowl. Jo inhaled a large mug of coffee and poured what was left in a to-go cup.

Now with caffeine in her system, she took a quick shower and dressed in faded blue jeans, a shirt with her father's store logo on it, and then slipped on her western style black boots. Moose impatiently waited for Jo to get herself together and started barking as she reached for her keys.

"Are you ready to go visit Wyatt this morning?"

Moose responded with another bark.

Frost covered the grass from the cool fall morning. Jo grabbed her jacket and large to-go cup of coffee as she headed for the door. She unlocked the front door to leave, and that is when she suddenly remembered about the intruder during the night. She shrugged it off as some teenager looking for a quick way to steal some cash. She opened the passenger side door on her truck and Moose didn't hesitate to jump in. He sat staring out the window as she drove to the hospital. He started to bark when she pulled into the hospital parking lot.

Jo snapped Moose's leash on his collar before opening the door. Moose followed her out the driver's side door and walked briskly toward the hospital entrance. "You need to slow down and behave or we won't be allowed back inside," Jo told Moose.

As if he understood, he stopped pulling and heeled perfectly by Jo's side. "Good boy," Jo said as she patted his head.

Jo quietly entered Wyatt's room in case he was asleep. Wyatt's eyes were closed, but opened as soon as Moose licked his hand.

"Sorry, I hope we didn't wake you."

"No, you didn't. The light bothers me so I was just resting my eyes. Thanks for bringing Moose back to visit."

"Moose was eager to see you this morning. How are you feeling?"

Wyatt rubbed his temples. "Other than feeling like a knife is piercing through my temple, I'm doing fine. The doctor is going to move me out of ICU and into a private room today. I'm going a little stir crazy and I'm ready to get out of this place."

"I'm sure the doctor wants to make sure you're out of danger before releasing you. Once you're moved to your new room, I'll check to see if I can leave Moose here with you for a little while."

"That would be great!" Wyatt continued to stroke Moose's head. "It's like a part of me is missing without him around."

"I know what you mean. He has hardly left my side since I found him. He's a very special dog. He even alerted me to someone trying to break into my house last night."

"Really? What happened?" Wyatt asked with concern in his voice.

"Oh, it was nothing, probably just some teenagers in the neighborhood."

"Did you see them?" Wyatt asked.

"No. All I saw was a dark colored Jeep Cherokee driving away by the time I reached the window and looked outside."

Wyatt suddenly became quiet and looked away.

Jo noticed his sudden change in mood. "Is everything okay?" she asked.

Wyatt focused back on Jo. "Yes. Thank you so much for taking care of Moose for me. I don't know what I would do if anything ever happened to him."

"Like I said, he has been a joy to have around. How long have you had him?"

"Almost six months now. He was given to me once I was released from rehab after being injured overseas."

"I'm sorry. I can't imagine what you went through in Afghanistan."

"As my therapist told me, we all have our demons which we must address. Moose has helped me combat mine."

"Is there anyone you would like to call to let them know where you are?"

"No, that's all right."

"Have you been able to remember who tried to kill you or why you were on Old Mill Pond Road?"

Wyatt became suddenly agitated. "No! I can't remember."

Jo thought his mood change was due to the fact he was just frustrated with himself.

The nurse walked in before Jo could say another word. "Are you ready to move to a room with a view?" the nurse asked.

Wyatt quickly returned to his friendly self. "Does it also have room service?" he joked.

"It comes with all the Jello you can eat," the nurse replied. "I'm going to raise you up a little higher in the bed and let you stabilize for a bit before moving you to the wheelchair. How is that? Are you experiencing any dizziness?"

Wyatt waited a few seconds before answering. "No, I'm good."

"I want you to slowly move your legs over the side of the bed and then lean on me so I can help support you before standing."

Jo moved herself in position next to the bed to help assist Wyatt, if needed.

Wyatt did as instructed. With the nurse on one side and Jo on the other, Wyatt rested his arms on their shoulders and stood up before sliding into the wheelchair.

"Very good," the nurse said. "Still no dizziness?" she asked.

"No, I'm fine."

"Jo, if you could grab Mr. Deckster's belongings in the night stand by the bed, we'll be on our way."

Jo opened the drawer and removed a wallet, old flip style cell phone, and belt. She looked around but that was all there was. She and Moose followed Wyatt in the wheelchair as the nurse wheeled him to his new temporary home. They turned into a brightly lit room. The sun was pouring in through the open blinds. Wyatt shielded his eyes from the painful light.

Jo saw Wyatt's distress and quickly closed the blinds. She helped the nurse get Wyatt into bed.

"How is your pain level?" the nurse asked.

"It's about a three," Wyatt responded, even though it was much worse.

The nurse seemed to sense his pain was more severe. "How about I give you something to help you rest?" She handed Wyatt a pill and glass of water.

Wyatt did as the nurse instructed. He took a drink of water and swallowed the pill. He leaned back in bed and tried to get comfortable.

Jo placed Wyatt's meager belongings in the night stand by the bed. "Would it be all right if I left Moose with Wyatt to keep him company?" Jo asked the nurse. "I'll come back in a few hours to pick him up."

The nurse hesitated, but saw the eager look on Wyatt's face. "I guess it would be okay as long as he doesn't make any noise and disturb the other patients."

Jo saw a smile cross Wyatt's face for the first time.

"Hear that boy? You can stay here with me." Wyatt roughed up Moose by rubbing him behind the ears.

Moose responded by licking Wyatt's hand.

The nurse left them alone. "I'll let you get some rest and come back at lunch to take Moose outside to do his business. Is there anything I can bring you?" Jo asked.

"No, I have everything I need right here." He motioned toward Moose and continued to pat him gently.

"I'll be back around one," Jo said as she left his room.

On the way to work Jo couldn't help but feel sorry for Wyatt. He didn't seem to have anyone else in his life but Moose. She wasn't sure she believed Wyatt when he said he couldn't remember who tried to kill him. She saw the look on his face and sudden change in mood. He's hiding something, but why wouldn't he want the police to find who did this to him? It made no sense. Jo pulled up to her father's auto parts store. There were already several cars in the parking lot, and she knew her Dad would be glad that she had finally arrived.

"Sorry Dad, for being late," she said as she rushed through the door.

"Where's Moose this morning?"

"I stopped by the hospital to check on Wyatt and left Moose with him."

"I've kinda gotten used to having him in the store during the day. No one would think about robbing us with him behind the counter."

"I know what you mean. I feel safer at night just knowing he's sleeping in the same room with me." She didn't want her Dad to worry and didn't mention the fact that Moose alerted her to an intruder last night.

Jo and her father stayed busy with customers all morning. She looked up at the clock and realized it was already after one. "Dad, I need to run by the hospital and check on Moose. Can I pick you up anything for lunch?"

"No, your Mom packed me a roast beef sandwich for lunch."

"I'll be back in about an hour."

Jo stopped by the diner on the way to the hospital and bought a large bowl of their famous chicken noodle soup. It was known to cure just about anything.

She quietly entered Wyatt's room and smiled at the sight of Moose in bed with Wyatt, both sound asleep.

Wyatt sensed a presence in the room and opened his eyes.

"I hope I didn't wake you." Moose lifted his head at the sound of her voice.

"No, I wasn't asleep. I was just resting my eyes."

"Are you hungry? I thought you might like something other than hospital food for lunch." Jo placed the bowl of soup on the tray by Wyatt's bed.

"It has to be better than the gruel the nurse has been trying to get me to eat."

Jo removed the plastic lid from the bowl. The steam carried the tantalizing smell to Wyatt's nose. "This chicken noodle soup is guaranteed to make you feel better."

"It smells awesome." Wyatt took a big spoonful. The look on his face said it all. "I may just live to see another day," he joked.

Moose started to drool all over the bedspread from the smell of food. "Why don't I take Moose outside while you finish your soup? I'll be right back." At the sight of his leash Moose jumped down from the bed and followed Jo outside. By the time she returned, Wyatt's bowl was empty.

"Thanks! That was just what I needed. Now if I could just persuade the doctor to let me leave."

"Already tired of your stay at the fine Wheeler Medical Center?" Jo asked.

"I start going a little stir crazy in confined spaces."

"Don't rush to get out of here too fast. You need to give your head a chance to heal. You were unconscious for quite some time. You need to concentrate on getting your strength back. Do you have someone to look after you once you are released?"

"Moose is all I need." Moose jumped back on Wyatt's bed and made himself comfortable as Wyatt stroked his head.

"You can always stay at my place until you are well enough to be on your own." Jo suddenly blurted out. "I have a spare bedroom and Moose is already comfortable with staying with me. It'll give you a chance to focus on getting well."

"I couldn't do that to you. You don't even know me. For all you know I could be an ax murderer," Wyatt joked.

"I have a pretty good read of people and doubt that you're an ax murderer. I may look weak and helpless, but I'm anything but."

"I have no doubt you can take care of yourself," Wyatt added.

"Then it's settled. You and Moose will stay with me until you've had a chance to recover." Before he could object, she added, "I've got to get back to work. I'll stop back by later this evening to pick up Moose."

Wyatt smiled to himself as he watched Jo leave. She was definitely a headstrong woman that liked getting her way. Wyatt had to be careful, though. He couldn't afford to get close to anyone right now. He needed to find the guy that tried to kill him first.

Chapter 5

Jo returned to the hospital that evening. This time Wyatt was awake, watching an old I love Lucy episode on the television when she entered his room. "You look like you are feeling better."

"The headache isn't as bad. I managed to walk two laps around the nurse's station."

"Well, aren't we ready to run a marathon!" Jo laughed.

"You joke, but when I was in the military I could outrun everyone in my unit. Running fifteen miles was like a walk in the park to me."

"I was never much for running, myself. It seemed like a lot of work to stay in shape. I get enough exercise maintaining my house and helping my Dad at his store. I'm sure you'll be passing everyone again soon," Jo encouraged.

"The nurse said if I can do five laps tomorrow the doc may let me leave."

"Fantastic! Have you thought any more about my offer to stay at my house?"

"I don't want to intrude. Moose and I will be okay on our own."

Jo was disappointed by his answer. "Are you sure? It won't be any trouble at all. I'm at work all day long, so you would have the place to yourself during the day to rest. And you know with any head injury you shouldn't be left alone for long periods of time without someone to check on you."

Wyatt had to admit she was persistent. He didn't really have any place to go. After Clark Davis passed away and the pizza place closed, he had to move out of the apartment above the restaurant. He had been doing odd jobs to make enough money to rent a room by the week. He didn't want to put Jo's life in danger, though. The intruder Jo mentioned could have been someone trying to find out what she knows. It might be safer for Jo, though, if he stayed close in case they decided to come back. "On second thought, if it's not too much trouble, maybe Moose and I can stay just a few days until I get my strength back."

"Great! I'll make up the guest room."

"If it will get me out of here tomorrow, I will force myself to do the five laps around the nurse's station no matter how difficult it is. I'm always up for a challenge."

"You seem to be the type of person to do what it takes to get better. I know you've been through this recovery process before, and I'm here to help you get back up on your feet. Don't hesitate to let me know if you need anything," Jo said. She realized Wyatt was not comfortable asking for help. There is so much he seemed to be hiding behind those deep sea blue eyes. She only hoped he would trust her enough to let her in. She looked at her watch. "I've got to get back to work. I'll stop back by tonight to pick up Moose."

Wyatt smiled to himself as she rushed out of the room. He wished circumstances were different. Jo seemed like the type of woman he would enjoy getting to know better.

***

The next morning Jo woke up early, excited at the thought of visiting with Wyatt before work. She managed to get herself together and take care of Moose in time to arrive at the hospital right at eight, when visiting hours began. Wyatt was awake and talking to the doctor when she entered his room.

"This man seems to think he's well enough to leave," the doctor told Jo. "I told him I would release him only if there was someone to keep an eye on him."

Jo spoke up. "Yes, that won't be a problem. I can take off work, if necessary, to help Wyatt recover."

"In that case, I will approve his release. If there are any signs of dizziness or nausea, make sure you call my office," the doctor said.

"You hear that boy? I get to go home with you," Wyatt told Moose.

The doctor left them alone. "I forgot to mention that I found your back pack behind the seat of your truck. Do you want me to bring you some clothes?"

"Yes. If you could get me my sweat pants and a t-shirt that would be great."

34

"I think I can manage that. Is there anything else you can think of?"

"No, that should be all I need for now. I should be out of your hair in a few days."

"You heard the doctor. You should not be left alone until your head has had a chance to heal."

Wyatt didn't want to argue, but didn't plan to stick around for long. He had a murderer to catch.

Jo left Moose with Wyatt while she prepared for his stay. She also explained everything to her Dad and made arrangements for her cousin to cover for her at work for a few days. She grew up next door to her cousin and he was more like a big brother to her. He owned a lawn care service which was slow during the winter months. He was more than happy to help out. She drove home and picked up the clothes Wyatt requested. Before returning to the hospital, she stopped at the store and picked up some food that Wyatt might like. She also found a pair of dark sunglasses to help shield the bright sunlight from his eyes. She quickly checked out, knowing Wyatt would be eagerly waiting for her to return so he could leave the hospital.

With clothes and sunglasses in hand, she entered Wyatt's room.

"I was starting to think you'd changed your mind."

"What, and leave Moose to put up with you all by himself? Never!" she joked.

Wyatt loved hearing Jo laugh.

"Here, try these on and see if they fit." Jo handed him the sunglasses she had purchased.

"You're an angel," Wyatt said as he carefully slid them on his head. He was now able to look toward the window without pain shooting through his head.

She handed him the clothes he requested. "Do you need any help changing?" Jo asked as she turned around to give Wyatt some privacy.

"No, I can manage." He pulled up the sweat pants which hung loosely on him after all the weight he had lost. Then he gently slipped the t-shirt over the bandage wrapped around his head. "Thanks for picking them up for me."

"No problem. Let me find a nurse to make sure you're free to escape this place. Then we can be on our way."

Jo returned a few minutes later with a nurse pushing a wheelchair. "You requested a ride?" the nurse asked jokingly.

Jo helped to steady Wyatt as he moved from the bed into the wheelchair. She grabbed his belongings from the night stand and placed them on Wyatt's lap. "Your taxi awaits," Jo said as they headed toward the exit with Moose walking closely by Wyatt's side.

The nurse waited at the door with Wyatt while Jo pulled her truck around.

Wyatt searched the parking lot for any signs that someone might be waiting for him to leave. He didn't see anyone suspicious, but it would be very easy for someone to conceal themselves behind one of many dark windshields, and be watching him now. He couldn't let his guard down. Someone may very well want to finish what they had started.

Jo pulled up to the curb in her truck and helped Wyatt into the passenger seat. Moose followed, sitting almost on top of Wyatt's lap.

"Moose, you can give him a little room. He's not going anywhere without you," Jo assured Moose.

"He's all right. I like having him close," Wyatt responded, giving Moose a big hug.

"I live about twenty minutes away so we should be there shortly. I know all this exertion is probably wearing you out."

Wyatt stayed alert. He kept an eye on the side mirror to make sure no one followed them. As they left the busy town streets he noticed a dark blue Jeep Cherokee in the distance. It stayed with them until Jo made the last turn toward her house. Wyatt wondered if he was just being paranoid, or whether someone was truly after him.

"Here we are!" Jo cheerfully announced. "It's not much, but I call it home. I had Burt park your beautifully restored truck underneath the carport to give it a little protection from the elements."

"Thanks for taking care of it for me."

"Now let's get you inside and in bed so you can get some rest." Jo walked around to the passenger side and held her arm out. "I'm stronger than I look, so lean on me for support so you don't fall."

Wyatt hated depending on anyone, but knew Jo would fuss if he didn't obey her command. He reached for her hand and slowly eased out of the truck. He stood for a few seconds to regain his balance. Jo slid her arm around his waist to help support him. If felt good to have her close, Wyatt thought to himself.

"You good?" Jo asked before starting to walk.

Wyatt smiled, "Yes, I'm good."

They slowly walked up the steps on the front porch and entered the house. Jo guided Wyatt to the guest room and pulled down the covers for him. He carefully sat on the edge of the bed.

"I'll take these off now that we're in the house." Jo removed the sunglasses from Wyatt's nose and set them on the night stand. The blinds were closed, allowing little light in the room to cause him any pain.

"Looks like Moose didn't waste anytime making himself comfortable," Wyatt said. Moose laid across the bed, leaving just enough room for Wyatt.

"Why don't you join him and I will make us some lunch? The doc said to keep it light for a few days, so I hope you don't mind some soup and your favorite, Jello." Jo laughed.

"That sounds good. I'm not that hungry, though."

After Jo left the room, Wyatt slid his sunglasses back on and eased over to the window. He cracked the blinds so he could look around outside. The street in front of the house was quiet. The nearest house appeared to be about a block away. There was no sign of the Jeep Cherokee that might have been following them. Convinced for now that he was safe, Wyatt made his way back to bed and climbed underneath the covers beside Moose. He sighed with relief as he laid his head on the pillow. The trip to the house had worn him out.

Jo quietly entered Wyatt's room with a bowl of soup. Wyatt was sound asleep. She was glad to see he was able to rest and not in too much pain. She gently closed the bedroom door as she left and placed the soup back in the pot on the stove. He could eat when he wakes up.

Jo rarely had a day off and didn't know what to do with herself. She called her Dad to check in to see how things were going at the store. "Hey, Dad. Are you managing to hold down the fort without me?"

"Your cousin Darrel and I are taking care of the business. How is Wyatt doing?"

"He's resting. The trip home really took it out of him."

"Your mother wants to drop off a chicken pot pie tonight to give you something good to feed Wyatt. Is it all right if we stop by after work?"

"Sure Dad, that would be nice. It would give you a chance to meet Wyatt." Jo knew that was the real motive in bringing supper.

Jo started a load of laundry, then switched on the television, turning the volume down low so as not to wake Wyatt. She channel surfed trying to find something of interest, and was just about to give up when one of the daytime talk shows caught her eye. A woman was trying to figure out who was the father of her child and the DNA test results were going to be revealed next. The soap opera like life of this woman was beyond belief as Jo listened intently. And the father of the child is…. Before Jo heard the answer, Wyatt yelled from the bedroom.

Jo rushed to Wyatt's side. He was having a nightmare. "Wyatt wakeup!" Jo yelled. She tried shaking him awake, but he sat up and threw her to the floor with such force that she sat stunned and shocked.

Wyatt opened his eyes and stopped thrashing about. He slowly remembered where he was.

"Are you all right?" Jo asked as she stood up and cautiously approached him. Wyatt was covered in sweat.

"Did I hurt you?" Wyatt asked out of breath.

"No, I'm fine. Let me get you a washcloth to help cool you down."

Jo returned with a damp, cool cloth and towel draped over her shoulder. Wyatt had laid back down and his eyes were fixed on the ceiling. "Here, you can use this to wash your face and neck."

Wyatt took the damp cloth and wiped his face with it, trying to remove the memories of his nightmare. He dried himself and tried to relax his tense muscles.

Jo pulled a chair up beside his bed, sensing his need for company. "You want to talk about it?" She asked, not sure it was her place to pry.

"I'm sorry. Sometime it's hard for me to distinguish between my nightmares and real life. I should have warned you to keep your distance when I'm sleeping."

"Nonsense. I've had intense dreams before that seemed so real. Even after I wake, it takes me awhile to realize it wasn't real. I can't imagine what you must be reliving in your dreams, but I'm sure it isn't pleasant. Would it help to talk about it?"

"Now you sound like my therapist," Wyatt tried to joke.

"I'm afraid I don't have any training in psychology, but I have been told I'm a good listener by the many customers that stop by to chat each day."

Wyatt smiled. "You do seem to have the ability to make people feel at ease around you. I'm sure they would tell you just about anything."

"You wouldn't believe the types of things people share with me. I could write a book about all the goings on in this town. For instance, Will told me he was working on the Hogan's tractor when he overheard Mrs. Hogan having a rendezvous in the hayloft, if you know what I mean."

Wyatt laughed, something he hadn't done much of lately. "I'm sure you could do just about anything you put your mind to."

"What is that supposed to mean?" Jo asked.

"From what little I know about you, you seem to be pretty self sufficient. Do you have a boyfriend?" Wyatt blurted out, not sure what possessed him to ask that.

"Let's just say I haven't had a lot of luck in that department. I think guys are intimidated by me, knowing more about cars than they do."

"I would think that would be a plus, having a mechanic around to help fix things when they break."

Jo was pleased with Wyatt's response. "How about you, do you have a girlfriend you are hiding somewhere?"

"No. After I left rehab I had just enough money to buy an old Ford Explorer that took me to Lory before it broke down. That's how I ended up working for Clark Davis at the pizza parlor and renting a room above his restaurant. I was just trying to survive and didn't have time to worry about dating anyone."

"What happened after Mr. Davis died?" Jo asked.

"I moved out and rented a room by the week, doing odd jobs, until I could figure out what I wanted to do next."

"So have you figured out what you want out of life?"

"Peace, that's what I really want, and to sleep all night without reliving the war in my head."

"Maybe I can help with that. Let's concentrate on getting your strength back and maybe we can work together to replace those horrible memories with some happy ones," Jo said as she looked into Wyatt's eyes. "To do that you need to eat. Can I talk you into eating a bowl of soup?"

Moose answered for Wyatt with a bark.

"Are you hungry?" Wyatt asked as he rubbed Moose's head.

"Two bowls of food it is. I'll be right back," Jo said.

Wyatt was starting to fall for Jo. He knew it was dangerous but couldn't stop himself. He yearned for a life of normalcy.

***

That evening, as promised, Jo's mother and father stopped by with a chicken pot pie and a chocolate cake. Jo opened the door, and before she had a chance to say a word, her mother blurted out, "Where is this boy that you found in the woods?"

"Mother, I'm sure Dad explained to you about me finding Moose in his truck and how his owner mysteriously disappeared. I was just glad I found Wyatt when I did. He's in the bedroom, resting. Let's put the food in the kitchen and I'll see if he's up to meeting you tonight. Just relax in the family room and I'll be right back."

Jo quietly opened the bedroom door. "I figured there was no way you could still be asleep after all the noise my mother made. Do you feel up to stretching your legs and meeting them? My mother can be a bit overbearing, but she means well."

"I need to get out of bed and walk, so now is as good a time as any," Wyatt replied. "I'm sure Moose could also use some exercise and would love to run around outside for a little while." At the sound of his name being mentioned, Moose barked to acknowledge he was ready to go.

"Come on Moose, let's go out," Jo said. Moose leaped off the bed and headed for the back door, tail wagging.

Jo returned to find Wyatt steadying himself against the bed. "Are you dizzy?" Jo asked.

"Just a little. Give me a second."

Jo watched as Wyatt used all of his strength to stand straight on his own and walk without assistance. Jo stayed close in case he stumbled. "Mom, Dad, I would like for you to meet Wyatt."

"Nice to meet you, son," Jo's Dad spoke up. "Jo told us about finding you shot, off Old Mill Pond Road. We have been praying for you to get better."

"Thank you, sir. Jo has been my guardian angel watching over me."

Jo helped Wyatt ease into a chair.

"Any idea who shot you?" her Mom asked.

"No ma'am. I'm afraid my memory of that day isn't real clear."

"Jo tells me you used to be in the military," her Dad said.

"Yes sir. I was in the Army and served for eight years."

"We thank you for your service. Any idea what you plan to do once you are well?" her Dad asked.

"No sir. I've just been trying to concentrate on getting better for now. Don't worry, I plan to leave as soon as I'm able to drive," Wyatt added.

"Dad, I think that is enough of the interrogation for now. Wyatt just left the hospital this morning and he needs his rest." Jo stood up to help Wyatt get up from the chair.

"It was nice meeting you. I know you are concerned about your daughter's well-being and I can assure you she's in good hands. I don't plan on taking advantage of her generosity, and I'm grateful for everything she has done for me. I will have to find a way to repay her kindness."

Jo helped Wyatt back to bed and then returned to her parents' stern faces.

"What do you know about this boy? I don't like you staying here by yourself with him in the house," her Mom said.

"Mom, he hardly has enough strength to get out of bed. I don't think you have anything to worry about," Jo said sarcastically.

"Come on, let's get home. I'm sure Jo will call if she needs anything," her Dad spoke up.

Jo opened the door for her parents. "Thanks for the food, Mom. I really do appreciate it."

Moose barked at the back door to let Jo know he was ready to come back in. Jo opened the door and Moose came barreling inside, full of energy and out of breath. "What have you been doing out there to get you so winded?" Jo glanced around the back yard but didn't see anything.

Moose proceeded to run to the bedroom to check on Wyatt, and Jo followed. "Sorry about the inquisition. They are really nice people once you get to know them."

"No, they were only showing how much they care for their daughter. I understand. They don't know anything about me and have no reason to trust me."

"But they should trust their daughter enough to know I can take care of myself," Jo said defensively. "Are you hungry? Mom brought an awesome looking chicken pot pie and a chocolate cake."

"I think I could eat a little," Wyatt said.

"Good. I'll be right back."

Jo moved her TV tray from the family room into Wyatt's room so she could eat with him. She normally ate by herself, while watching television, after work. It's nice to have someone to eat with for a change, Jo thought.

"It smells delicious," Wyatt said as Jo handed him a plate of food.

She set a glass on the night stand. "I brought you some ginger ale. My Mom always used to give it to me to drink when I was sick, to help ease my stomach. Moose, I didn't forget you." Jo placed a bowl with a little pot pie in it for Moose on the floor. He didn't hesitate jumping off the bed and diving into his bowl.

"Well, I guess he approves of your Mom's cooking!" Wyatt laughed.

While they ate, Jo probed, to find out more about Wyatt. "Are your parents still alive?"

"I'm not sure. I was raised in a foster home. That's one reason I joined the military when I turned eighteen."

"Oh, I'm sorry."

"There's nothing to be sorry about. That's just how it was. My Mom had a drug problem and I'm not even sure she knew who my father was."

"How about your foster parents? Were they good people?"

"I moved around to several homes from the time I was five until I was eighteen. I never really let myself get too attached to anyone."

"Do you know if you have any brothers or sisters?"

"I don't think so. My Mom was eventually incarcerated shortly after I was placed in foster care. I never had any contact with her after that."

"Do you ever wonder if she cleaned herself up and got help?"

"No, not really. I figured if she wanted to see me, she could have found me. Don't get me wrong. I accepted my fate years ago and don't hold a grudge for what she did. Staying mad at her won't change anything, or help me."

"Wow, I'm impressed. I don't know that I could have been so forgiving."

"You never know how you will handle a situation until you experience it first hand," Wyatt said.

Jo thought there was a much deeper meaning in what he was saying. He wasn't just talking about his mother. "I know you must be exhausted. Let me clear the dishes out of your way so you can get some rest. I'll leave some water by your bed so if you get thirsty in the middle of the night you won't have to get up."

"Thanks for everything, Jo. I really do appreciate it."

"No problem. I'm just happy to know I can help. Holler if you need anything. Sweet dreams." Jo closed the door and went to the kitchen to clean up the dirty dishes. As she placed the plates in the dishwasher, she thought about how difficult growing up with no real parents must have been for him. No wonder he has no one in his life. He has never given anyone a chance to get close.

Chapter 6

Jo woke from a deep sleep. She thought she heard a noise coming from the other room. At first she wasn't sure if she had just dreamed it. She laid still for a minute, listening intently. Then she heard the front door close. After the incident last night, she wasn't going to take any chances. She grabbed her rifle from the back of her closet and tiptoed through the house. All seemed quiet. She approached the front door and noticed it was unlocked. She eased the door open, trying not to make a sound. She searched the front yard for the source of the noise. Then she noticed a light come on inside Wyatt's pickup truck. Before she could determine who was inside the truck, the light went out. With her rifle pressed against her shoulder, she approached from the rear of the truck so she wouldn't be seen. The truck door suddenly opened and a man stepped out. "Freeze or I'll blow your head off!" she yelled.

"Don't shoot! It's me." Wyatt slowly turned around.

Jo lowered her rifle. "Wyatt, what in blazes are you doing out here in the middle of the night? I almost shot you."

"I remembered I had a gun hidden in the floorboard of the truck and wanted to check to see if it was still there." Wyatt held up the 9 mm handgun in his right hand.

"That couldn't wait until morning?"

"I feel more comfortable knowing I have a weapon close by."

Jo wasn't sure that was a good thing, but understood the need to feel more secure by having control of your own destiny. "Where's Moose?"

"I told him to stay and closed the bedroom door so he wouldn't make any noise."

Just like when you left him in the truck, Jo thought to herself. Moose wouldn't disobey a command from Wyatt. "Let's get you back inside before you catch a cold," Jo said with concern in her voice.

Wyatt looked over at Jo and smiled.

44

Jo realized she was only wearing a large t-shirt, and pulled it down a little. "I didn't have time to put on any pants," she exclaimed. Thank goodness Wyatt couldn't see her blushing in the dark, she thought.

Wyatt put his arm around Jo's neck for support. Once back in bed he set his 9 mm gun on the night stand within reach. "Good boy!" he told Moose to reward him for following his command to stay in the room. He hugged Moose lovingly.

"How is your pain? Do you need another pain pill or anything to drink or eat before I return to bed?"

"No, I'm good. Sorry to wake you with such a fright. I promise I have no intention of leaving my room for the rest of the night," Wyatt said, giving her a two figure salute to show he was serious.

"Sweet dreams. I'll see you in the morning," Jo responded with a smile as she returned to her bedroom. She set the rifle up against the wall beside her bed. She had this uneasy feeling that wouldn't go away. She tossed and turned for at least an hour before she started to drift back to sleep. That's when rapid gunfire erupted. Bullets were flying everywhere. Jo hit the floor, lying as flat as possible as the bullets ricocheted throughout the house. The firing stopped after what seemed like an eternity but was probably only thirty seconds. Jo grabbed her rifle and bumped into Wyatt in the hall.

"Are you all right?" Wyatt asked.

"I'm fine. What about you and Moose?" Jo asked.

That's when Wyatt realized Moose wasn't by his side. They rushed back to Wyatt's bedroom. Moose was lying on the floor whimpering. Wyatt dropped to his knees to see how bad he was wounded. "He's bleeding from his hip. Is there a veterinary hospital close by that we can take him to?" Wyatt lifted Moose, a hundred pound dog, without hesitation.

Jo grabbed her jeans at the end of the bed and slid them on as she rushed to her truck. She opened the passenger door for Wyatt. He gently placed Moose across the truck seat and slid underneath his head to hold him tight. Jo broke all speed limits driving to the twenty four hour animal hospital located about fifteen miles away. Jo's speedometer hit sixty as she drove through the downtown area, not slowing down for the one red light. Luckily, at this hour of night there were few cars to worry about. She skidded to a stop by the entrance. Jo jumped out of the truck and ran around to the passenger side to help Wyatt lift Moose. Moose was still whining and in a lot of pain. The staff on duty directed them to an examination room and Wyatt placed Moose's limp body on the table. Wyatt quickly explained to the veterinarian on duty that Moose had been shot in the hip. "It's going to be okay. Hang in there, boy," Wyatt said as he rubbed Moose's massive head.

"I need you to wait outside while I work on Moose. I'll have someone status you as soon as we determine the extent of his injuries," the vet directed.

Jo and Wyatt took a seat by the front reception desk. Wyatt looked toward the floor, with his arms resting on his legs, trying to control his emotions.

"Moose is a strong, heathy dog. He'll recover," Jo said trying to sound encouraging.

Wyatt didn't say a word, and kept his eyes turned away from Jo.

"I'd better call Charlie, the sheriff, to let him know about the shooting. Maybe it's not too late to catch whoever did this. Did you by any chance see anything?"

"No. By the time the firing stopped, I jumped up and looked out the window, but they were long gone," Wyatt said.

Jo pulled her cell phone out of her pocket and dialed Charlie's number, which she now knew by heart. "Charlie, it's Jo. I'm so sorry to wake you, but someone just shot up my house. Wyatt was in my guest room and neither of us were injured, but Moose was shot. We're at the vet's waiting to hear his prognosis."

Charlie was very concerned and assured her he would check out her place immediately.

Jo ended the call and relayed their conversation to Wyatt, "Charlie is going to meet us here after stopping by my place first. Do you think this shooting has anything to do with who tried to murder you?" Jo asked.

Wyatt continued looking at the floor, anger now showing on his face. "That's what I'm thinking. I never meant to put you in any danger. Moose and I will leave as soon as he is able."

"Don't be ridiculous. You are still recovering from a head injury and I'm sure Moose is going to need some time to heal. You need to tell the sheriff what you know, so he can catch this person!" Jo said, now upset.

"I can't do that," Wyatt said softly.

"What do you mean you can't do that?"

"I don't know who is trying to kill me."

"You must have some idea what this is about and why someone would want you dead," Jo insisted.

Wyatt didn't say a word. Frustrated, Jo got up and stormed outside to get some fresh air. How could she help him if he wasn't willing to help himself? Jo paced just outside the double glass doors, in the cool night air, while she waited for news on Moose. She watched as Wyatt didn't move from his seat inside, and continued to stare at the floor. "How can he remain so calm?" she said out loud. Finally, one of the veterinary assistants approached Wyatt. Jo rushed back inside to hear the report.

"The bullet shattered Moose's hip. The doctor is still working on him now to try to reinforce the hip bone the best he can to give Moose the best chance at a full recovery. I'll return once Moose is out of surgery and in recovery."

"Well, that's good news. It doesn't sound like his injuries are life-threatening, and he has a chance of a full recovery," Jo said.

Before Wyatt could say anything, Charlie walked into the room. "You weren't kidding when you said someone shot up your house. Either one of you care to share who may have done this?" Charlie looked directly at Wyatt.

"I don't know if this is anything, but last night I woke to find my window open in the family room. I know I didn't open it, and Moose alerted me to an intruder. When I looked outside all I saw was a dark Jeep Cherokee speeding away."

Wyatt spoke next. "I also thought I saw a dark blue Jeep Cherokee following us home from the hospital yesterday, but I wasn't sure if I was just imagining it."

"Well, that's a start. What time did you leave the hospital yesterday?" Charlie asked.

"I think it was about eleven in the morning," Jo responded.

"I'll check the security cameras around town for any footage of a dark blue Jeep Cherokee that may have been caught on camera around eleven, to see if I can make out the license plate. I'll let you know if I discover anything. Wyatt, do you know of any reason why someone may want you dead?" Charlie asked.

"No sir," Wyatt responded.

"Very well. If you remember anything, give me a call. How's Moose doing?" Charlie asked with the concerned look of a friend.

"He was shot in the hip, but it sounds like he should recover," Jo said.

"Good. Jo, you may want to give Butch a call. He should be able to repair the damage made from the bullets to your house. It looks like you will need to replace the glass in two windows and plug about fifty holes in your walls."

"I'll definitely do that, Charlie. Thanks for your help," Jo said.

The sun was now starting to come up. Before Jo could say another word, the doctor approached.

"Moose is doing well and is in recovery. I removed the bullet and secured the broken hip bone to give it a chance to heal. Dogs are much more resilient than humans. They never stop amazing me at how quickly they can recover. That's not to say he won't experience any pain, just that he will tolerate it better than a human. He'll need to stay here for a couple of days just to make sure there are no complications from the surgery. Then I'll give you instructions for keeping his wound clean and limiting his movement to give the bone a chance to mend."

"Can I see him?" Wyatt asked.

"He's still waking up from the anesthesia and may be a little disoriented. If you would like to go back for a few minutes to help comfort him, you can."

Wyatt and Jo followed the doctor. Moose was lying on a table with his right hind leg bandaged to a splint to limit its movement. Wyatt gently stroked Moose's head to assure him he was by his side. "It's all right, buddy. You'll be chasing squirrels again before you know it. I'm right here with you."

Jo watched Wyatt and Moose as a tear came to her eye. Everything that had happened was starting to sink in. She couldn't stand to see any animal in pain. She knew how much Moose meant to Wyatt and her heart ached for him.

One of the veterinary assistants came over. "He's going to be resting most of the day. Don't worry, I'll keep an eye on him for you and administer pain medicine as needed to help him stay calm. You can come back later this afternoon to visit for a little while, if you like. We find dogs recover faster if their owners aren't present. They seem to sense their mood and won't relax when they're around."

Wyatt took the hint and reluctantly left. They returned to the truck. The sun was now up and Wyatt shielded his eyes from the bright light.

"I think I have a spare pair of sunglasses in the glove box," Jo said as she opened it and dug around. "Voila! They may be a little small, but will help shield your eyes from the sunlight," Jo said.

"Pink, just my color," Wyatt managed to joke at the sight of the glasses.

Jo looked over at Wyatt in the bright pink sunglasses with white flowers on the rim and laughed. Then she noticed a trickle of blood running down Wyatt's face. "Wyatt, you're bleeding! You must have opened your wound back up. I'm going to run you by the hospital to make sure you are all right."

"No, don't!" Wyatt used his hand to put pressure on his head to stop the bleeding. "They'll just want to admit me again and I can't take that right now. Just take me to your house and I'll get a clean bandage and keep pressure on it until it stops bleeding. I'll be fine."

Jo wasn't convinced, but she was too tired to argue. She drove home and they approached cautiously. There were splinters of wood and glass everywhere. "Be careful. I'll sweep up the glass as soon as we get your head re-bandaged and stop the bleeding. Then I'll call Butch to see when he can start the repairs."

"This is all my fault. I'll pay whatever it takes to fix it," Wyatt said apologetically.

"We'll worry about that later. You must be about to drop from exhaustion. Why don't you make yourself comfortable in the recliner in the family room? I'll get some warm water and a towel and be right back so I can clean your wound and place a fresh bandage over it."

Wyatt did as instructed, reclining the chair back, and resting his achy head against the headrest. Jo returned with her hands full of medical supplies. She tenderly removed the bandage from Wyatt's head and gently cleaned the wound.

Wyatt winced in pain.

"Sorry, I know it must hurt. Can you hold this gauze against your head while I secure it in place?"

Wyatt did as instructed, without saying a word.

"Now that looks better." Jo admired her work. "Are you hungry?" Jo asked.

"No. My head is throbbing. Just let me lie here a little while with my eyes closed."

"How about a few extra strength Tylenol so you can get some rest?" Jo asked. She didn't wait for a response. She retrieved a glass of water and gave him three pills to help with the pain.

He swallowed the pills without hesitation and laid his head back against the cushion.

Jo quietly went into the kitchen and called Butch to see when he could start patching up her house. She was glad to hear he could arrive after lunch. She looked at the clock and couldn't believe it was only nine in the morning. She made herself a pot of strong coffee. While she waited for the coffee to stop dripping, she noticed Moose's food bowl on the floor. The house seemed oddly empty without Moose underfoot.

With a large dose of caffeine now in her system, Jo started picking up the debris the best she could. Most of the damage was to the front of the house, which included Wyatt's bedroom and the hallway. She removed the bloodstained rug where Moose had laid bleeding. She threw it in the garbage. She swept up the glass and debris from the worn hardwood floors in the foyer and bedrooms. She found some plywood in the shed out back and tried to quietly nail the boards over the broken windows.

She was just about finished cleaning when she heard Wyatt scream, "Rob, stop!" She rushed into the family room to find Wyatt thrashing about in his sleep. She approached with caution after what happened the last time she tried to wake him from a nightmare. She firmly shook his arm and yelled, "Wyatt, wake up! You're having another bad dream."

Wyatt opened his eyes. His body was still in a defensive position, ready to strike.

"You're safe Wyatt. It was just another nightmare," Jo said with tenderness in her voice.

Wyatt slowly returned to the present and rubbed the memory of the nightmare from his face. "I'm sorry."

"There is nothing to apologize for. You were yelling out the name Rob. Is that someone you served with?"

Wyatt hesitated before answering. "Yeah, he was in my unit."

"Did something happen to him?"

"Yes," was all Wyatt said.

"I'm sorry. Do you have the same nightmare where you're trying to stop Rob or are there others?"

"Most of the time it's the same nightmare. It's like I'm trying to change the past. Until I figure out a way to change the outcome, I think I'll continue to see the event over and over in my mind every time I sleep."

"Maybe if you talk about it you can get to a point where you accept the outcome."

"I don't know. I don't think you really want to hear about my war stories."

"I have watched every war movie ever made. I'm sure what you experienced can't be worse than the blood and gore I've seen on the movie screen. What do you have to lose? At worse you continue having the nightmare, and at best you may get a good night of rest without waking up in terror."

Wyatt thought for a minute, trying to gather his thoughts before he proceeded. "First you have to understand that what I'm about to tell you may just be my imagination. I have no way to verify if what I'm dreaming ever really happened, or if it is just something my mind has made up. I lost most of my memory of the events that occurred the day I was injured in Afghanistan."

"I understand, but I believe our subconscious memories are just that. That doesn't mean what you are remembering happened in the exact way you dream, but that at least portions of it may be true in your own mind. So with that being said, what do you dream every time you sleep?"

"The dream always starts with my unit on patrol. Rob is sitting beside me in our Humvee. He is joking about what's the first thing he's going to do when he gets home, take a warm shower for a very long time. It's suddenly dark. There's no moon and it's pitch black outside, other than the stars that fill the night sky. It's so serene, but I feel death is all around me. Our convoy stops. Now we're on foot approaching a building. I tense in anticipation that something bad is about to happen. Rob is in front of me with his M-16 raised as we enter the building. It's too quiet. I try to stop Rob from going inside the building, but he disappears through the entrance. I rush to catch up with him but don't make it in time. A loud explosion throws my body through the air like a rag doll. My body is on fire. I lift my head up from the ground and see children playing in the field in front me. It's now daylight. They are joyfully playing, kicking a soccer ball around the dry field. In my dream I try to warn them, but I can't move. I watch as bombs explode all around them. That's when I wake up."

"You said you received your head injury in an explosion. Were you told if other people were injured, or where the explosion occurred?"

"No, just that a bomb went off close to me, that I was stabilized, then transported to a military hospital where surgeons operated on me to remove the shrapnel from my skull."

"Do you know if Rob was with you and whether he survived?"

"No. I was provided very little information when I awoke from my coma. I was totally out of it for almost a month. I had to be retrained to walk, talk, and eat. I have no memory of the events that lead to my injuries. The hospital staff told me what little they knew, which was that my unit was attacked and that an explosion caused my injuries, but that's about it. Their main focus was on therapy so I could take care of myself again."

"After you recovered did you try to contact anyone in your old unit?"

Wyatt hesitated. "Yes, I was able to track down my old commander. But he wasn't very helpful or eager to discuss what happened. He said it was classified."

52

"You told me this all happened about a year ago. Have you tried to search for any news footage on soldiers or civilians being injured in an explosion in Afghanistan?"

"No, I hadn't even considered that. There were always reporters at our post, but they normally didn't follow us on our missions."

"Let me do a search on my cell phone for Afghanistan, explosion and see how many hits I get."

Wyatt waited while Jo tapped away on her cell phone screen and eagerly watched as she scrolled through the list that appeared. "Well, did you find anything?" Wyatt impatiently asked.

"Yes, there are two news stories from about a year ago. One you will find interesting. A school was accidentally bombed, killing many women and children. The Taliban is believed to be responsible for the bombing. Here is another story that indicates Americans were thought to have been in proximity of the school and were possibly the intended target for the bomb. No one has come forward to claim responsibility."

"Do you see anything about Americans being injured around the same time?"

"There are a couple of stories detailing that heavy gunfire was exchanged and a story which indicates soldiers retook some of the ISIS territories. No causalities are listed, though." Jo looked up from her phone. "We at least have a start. The nightmare you're having about the children in the field being killed by an explosion could mean you were close when it happened. Maybe that's the bomb blast that injured you."

Wyatt struggled to remember anything from the day he was hurt. "I just don't remember. Maybe I read it somewhere or saw something on the news about it. Maybe that's why it's stuck in my head."

"I think it's much more likely that you lived it. Viewing such a traumatic event had to have made an impact on your brain. You just don't forget something like that. Versus if you read about it, your brain would just categorize it as another tragic event in someone else's life. It wouldn't have near the same affect and wouldn't cause you to recall the event over and over," Jo said.

"Have you ever thought about becoming a psychologist?" Wyatt joked.

"Very funny. I'm just speaking from events in my life that have stuck with me over time. For instance, when I was eight years old, I was playing at the park just down the street from my house, without a care in the world. Suddenly I heard the screeching of tires and the horrible, loud sound of metal crashing. I looked up and watched as a car flew through the air and landed upside down in the street by the park. I ran to the vehicle to see if I could help. I remind you, I was only eight years old. When I arrived, I saw a bloody arm hanging out the driver's side window and a woman on the passenger side was screaming from pain. By this time other cars had stopped to help, so I just stood there watching the events unfold in front of me in slow motion. But even to this day, I can still clearly see the blood everywhere and the pain stricken look on the woman's face. It was months before I felt safe to ride in a car again. Emotional events do a strange thing to our brain and won't let us forget."

"So it's possible that I was at the school when it was bombed. So now what?"

"Now we try to track down Rob," Jo said.

"Before you get yourself too involved in my past, you need to consider that this is why someone is trying to kill me. There is something I haven't shared with you or the police. The reason I was on Old Mill Pond Road is because I received a text from a phone number I didn't recognize. It said meet me at the pond on Old Mill Pond Road to get the answers you search for."

"You didn't think this was worth mentioning before?" Jo said angrily.

"I didn't want anyone else to get hurt. I figured as soon as I was well enough I would track down who sent me the text and take care of it myself," Wyatt said.

"What do you mean by 'take care of it myself'? Are you planning on killing the person?"

"I just know this person might be able to provide me with some answers. I would figure the rest out later."

"And what if this person has no intention of telling you anything, and just wants you dead so you can't drag up something in the past that is best left forgotten?" Jo asked.

"That's a possibility and I plan to cross that junction when I come to it. I've relied on myself for such a long time and didn't see a need to put anyone's else's life at risk."

"How's that working for you?" Jo asked a little angrily.

Wyatt rolled his eyes at Jo. The doorbell rang, ending their conversation.

"Butch must be here to start repairs," Jo announced. She opened the front door, which looked more like Swiss cheese than a door. "Hey Butch, how are you doing?"

"Much better than you, obviously. Who did you piss off?" Butch asked.

Jo didn't want to take the time to try to explain and replied, "No telling. Can you repair all the damage?"

Butch looked at the outside wall and whistled. "Man, this guy must have really been furious with you. Yeah, it looks like I'll have to replace a few pieces of siding and the glass in the two windows that are damaged. I should be able to use some wood putty to plug the holes in the front door. I might be able to finish it by tomorrow if I can find the glass and siding in stock. Do you want me to repair the sheetrock inside the house?"

"No, I can take care of that myself. I should be here till around four, if you need anything. After that, call me on my cell."

"Will do. Let me run to the store for a few supplies and I'll be right back," Butch said as he returned to his old beat up truck that looked like it had seen better days.

Since they hadn't had breakfast, Jo heated up some leftover chicken pot pie for lunch. Regardless of Wyatt's insistence that he wasn't hungry, he managed to eat a bowl full. With their stomachs content, Jo stretched out on the sofa next to Wyatt, who was still relaxing in the recliner. Within minutes they both fell asleep after their exhaustive night. It didn't seem long before they were woken by the sound of Butch hammering outside.

After rubbing the sleep from her eyes, Jo said, "There'll be no more rest for us here. Do you feel up to checking on Moose?"

"Yes, let me take a quick shower first. I still smell like the antiseptic from the hospital."

While Wyatt cleaned up, Jo drank a caffeinated soda to help clear her mind. She looked in the mirror and hardly recognized the tired face with the crazed hair that stared back at her. She quickly put on some clean clothes, washed her face, brushed her hair and teeth, and applied a little makeup to cover the dark circles under her eyes. "Hopefully I won't scare anyone now," she said to herself.

Wyatt appeared dressed in jeans and a clean black t-shirt. He had shaved and his chiseled jaw line was much more prominent. "Well, don't you smell better!" Jo laughed.

"I feel a lot better also, getting that hospital smell off of me. You don't look too bad yourself. Are you ready to go?"

Jo was thrilled that Wyatt had noticed the effort she had made to look nice, and secretly hoped he would stay a part of her life for a while.

Chapter 7

Moose was awake when they arrived at the veterinarian's. He wagged his tail at the sight of Wyatt. He was lying on a heavy comforter placed inside a kennel on the floor. The door to the kennel was open, so Wyatt sat on the floor to get down to his level so he could be close to Moose.

Jo stood next to Wyatt and leaned down to gently pat Moose on the head. "How are you doing, boy?"

Moose whimpered in response.

"I know you don't feel too good right now. Hopefully you can come home with me tomorrow," Wyatt said.

The veterinary assistant spoke up, "Maybe you can get him to drink some water and eat a little."

"I have just the thing for you." Wyatt pulled some bacon favored treats from his pocket. "These are your favorite, aren't they boy?" Wyatt held one up to Moose's nose and he suddenly became much more interested in eating. Moose sat up, eyeing the treats in Wyatt's hand. He handed him one and Moose gobbled it up, swallowing without even chewing. "That tasted pretty good, didn't it?" Wyatt handed him a few more.

Jo handed Wyatt a bowl half full of water. "Here, try and see if you can get him to drink."

Wyatt slid the bowl in front of Moose. At first he didn't want anything to do with it and turned his head away. "Come on boy, you can drink just a little." Wyatt leaned over the bowl and pretended to drink out of it while Moose watched intently.

That did the trick. Moose leaned over and cautiously took a lick. "That's a good boy," Wyatt praised him as he drank all the water without stopping.

Next, he set a small amount of moist beef flavor canned dog food in front of Moose. After taking a bite and determining that it was edible, he devoured the entire full bowl within seconds flat. Moose looked up from his empty bowl after licking it clean to get every last drop of food.

"Sorry, boy. That's all I can give you for now. Let's see how that sets on your stomach and then you can have more later." After his meal, Moose was given some pain medicine. Wyatt gently caressed his smooth coat until Moose fell back asleep.

"He should rest soundly through the night. Don't worry, I'll be here all night to keep an eye on him," the veterinary assistant spoke up.

Reluctantly, Wyatt and Jo left Moose to rest. On the way back to the truck Jo said, "I could sure use a burger, chocolate milkshake, and fries to cheer me up. How does that sound to you?"

"That actually sounds pretty good after the bland food I've been forced to eat," Wyatt said.

Jo drove to Stacy's diner and they found an empty booth along the wall. They slid across from each other and made themselves comfortable. Their order was delivered quickly, and they ate slowly, savoring every fat laced bite. They took their time, for neither was eager to return home with the reminder of what had happened still evident around the house. As they were finishing their meal, Jo's cell phone rang.

"It's Charlie!" Jo whispered over to Wyatt. "Hey Charlie, did you find the vehicle of the person responsible for shooting up my house?"

"As a matter of fact, I did. I was able to get a license plate number off the bank's security camera footage. I sent out a BOLO to all the officers in the area and it was spotted in the Walmart parking lot. The owner was nowhere in sight. I had an officer stake out the vehicle, but no one ever returned. So either the vehicle was abandoned there or the driver spotted us and took off. It has been towed to the impound lot while I wait for the search warrant to be approved. Do you and Wyatt have a second to stop by my office?"

"Sure, we're just down the street in the diner. We'll be there in a few minutes."

Jo filled Wyatt in on the vehicle being found. They quickly ate the rest of their fries and washed them down with their milkshakes before leaving for the police station.

They entered Charlie's sparsely furnished office and he motioned for them to have a seat in the chairs placed in front of his desk.

Wyatt eagerly asked, "Did you discover who the vehicle belongs to?"

"First, let me ask you a few questions. Do you recognize this person?" Charlie turned his computer screen around and showed Wyatt a photograph.

"Yes, that's Rob Manocini. He served with me in Afghanistan. What does the vehicle have to do with him?"

"Would he have any reason to want to kill you?" Charlie asked.

"No, not at all. Rob served with me in the military. We watched each others's backs for almost eight years before I was injured. I thought he might have been killed the same day I received my injuries. I'm thrilled to hear he's still alive."

"I'm not sure if he's alive, but the vehicle we found matching your description is registered to him. It's possible someone stole his vehicle and drove it here on purpose so we couldn't trace it back to whoever actually tried to kill you. We were able to look at security camera footage from Walmart. The vehicle pulled into the lot early this morning, probably just after shooting up your house. The occupant got out of the vehicle and walked out of the view of the camera. The person was wearing a baseball cap so we didn't get a clear image of their face. Once the search warrant is approved, we'll search the vehicle and dust for any prints. If we are lucky, hopefully we can get a hit."

"This just doesn't make any sense," Jo spoke up. "Why would Rob, or someone who knew Rob, want Wyatt dead?"

Wyatt remained quiet, trying to come up with an explanation, but nothing came to mind.

"Thanks, Charlie, for letting us know what you found," Jo said. "It's late and I know your wife is probably waiting up for you to get home."

"She's used to my odd hours and will survive. You two be careful. Whoever tried to kill you last night may try again tonight once they figure out they weren't successful. I will have a cruiser drive by your neighborhood throughout the night to watch for anything out of the ordinary."

"I appreciate that," Jo said as they left Charlie's office.

Wyatt was quiet all the way back to Jo's house. Jo knew when to keep her mouth closed and let him think in peace. When they arrived home they were pleased to find the holes in the front door had been patched while they were gone and it had been made solid once again. There were several pieces of new white vinyl siding lying on the ground in front of the house. The two windows were still boarded up with the plywood that Jo had nailed in place that morning.

Once inside, they both plopped on the sofa from exhaustion. Jo turned on the television and found a show on about the Alaskan wilderness. Neither spoke, deep in their own thoughts. The show quickly had Jo falling asleep, but she didn't want to be alone. She fell asleep against Wyatt's shoulder next to her on the sofa. He eased out from underneath her and gently covered her with a blanket so she wouldn't get cold. He tried to ignore the urge he had to want to take care of her forever. He kept his 9 mm close and forced himself to stay awake just in case another attempt was made on his life. He was determined to not to let them get away again.

Wyatt watched the late show as he fought exhaustion. He knew if he allowed himself to sleep, the nightmare would return. He thought about what Sheriff Charlie had told him. How could Rob's Jeep Cherokee be following him? If any part of his recurring nightmare was true, Rob didn't make it home from Afghanistan. His horrible dream always ended with the same feeling that the world was coming down all around him and everything going dark. He went over in his mind what little he remembered of the day he was injured. He tried to recall every little detail. It was difficult to separate reality from his nightmares. He glanced over at Jo, happy to see her finally sleeping soundly. She was truly beautiful inside and out. She acted all tough, but he knew deep inside it was all an act to cover up her insecurities. He would love to be able to stay and protect her for the rest of his life, but knew that was impossible.

***

Just as Wyatt was giving in to sleep, he heard a noise. He slowly lifted his head just in time to see a flash of light outside the window. He quietly got up from the recliner and reached for his 9 mm resting on the end table. He walked without making a sound and snuck out the back kitchen door to surprise whoever was outside. He peeked around the side of the house and witnessed someone with a flashlight standing beside his truck. Using his military training, he crept up behind the person without being seen or heard. "Don't move or I'll blow your brains out!"

The perpetrator obeyed and stood perfectly still.

"Now raise your hands so I can see them." Wyatt stared at the object held in the intruder's right hand. At first Wyatt couldn't make it out. Then he realized it was grenade. Before he could say another word, the intruder tossed the grenade inside the open truck door, then took off running. Wyatt leaped around the back of the house in an attempt to block the impact from the explosion.

Within seconds, the grenade exploded. A large ball of fire shot into the air the height of the old oak tree located along the side of the yard. Pieces of his truck filled the air. Flaming debris came raining down from the sky. Wyatt raced to grab the garden hose lying near the back steps and opened the nozzle all the way. He shot water up the roof of the house to extinguish the burning debris before the roof caught on fire.

"Wyatt, where are you?" Jo yelled!

"I'm back here," Wyatt managed to say over the roaring flames.

Jo ran around toward the sound of Wyatt's voice and was relieved to see him, hose in hand, dousing the flames. "Are you all right? What happened?"

"Yes, I'm fine, but the guy that did this got away!" Wyatt said angrily.

"Let me call Charlie and the fire department. It might not be too late to catch him," Jo said as she pressed call on her cell phone.

A police cruiser pulled up before Jo got off the phone, with the sound of sirens from the fire department close behind. Jo extinguished the glowing embers around her house while Wyatt talked to the officer.

"The man that did this is wearing a baseball cap, jeans, and dark colored shirt. He ran in that direction," Wyatt said as he pointed down the street. "It has only been about five minutes, so he couldn't have gotten far," Wyatt hurriedly explained to the officer.

The police cruiser dashed off in the direction Wyatt had indicated as the sound of sirens from the fire truck grew closer.

The firemen quickly took charge upon arriving and extinguished the remains of the flames on the truck before they could destroy the house. The damage was confined to the carport area. The siding on that side of the house was a little singed from the heat, but the house was undamaged. There was nothing left of Wyatt's truck but a melted mass of smoldering metal.

Jo and Wyatt sat on the front steps and watched with exhausted stares as the firemen put away their gear. Wyatt held his head in his hands to try to stop the throbbing. Darkness surrounded them now, with the flames extinguished. The dim porch light illuminated the destruction.

Jo, overcome with emotion, grabbed Wyatt's hand. "When I heard the explosion and woke to find you missing, I thought you were dead."

"I saw a light outside your family room window and went outside to investigate the source." He lifted his t-shirt to show Jo he had his 9 mm gun stuck in the back of his jeans. "I saw a guy open the door of my truck and I quietly approached so he wouldn't hear me coming. I jabbed my gun into his back and told him to put his hands in the air, where I could see them. That's when I realized the guy had a grenade in his right hand. The pin had already been removed and he was holding the trigger with his thumb. He tossed it in my truck and took off running before I could do anything. I had to take cover, and wasn't able to stop him."

"I'm so sorry about your truck. I know how much it meant to you, being it was a gift from Clark Davis. Let me look at your head and make sure your wound didn't open back up," Jo said with concern in her voice.

Wyatt relented and let Jo remove the soot covered bandage from his head, knowing she would not leave him alone until she was sure he was fine. He hated to admit to himself, but he liked having someone close who cared for him.

"It looks okay, but we need to go inside and clean it before it gets infected," Jo said.

A police cruiser pulled up just as they were dragging themselves off the front steps. Charlie approached. "I have a suspect in the back of my cruiser. I want you to take a look and let me know if you recognize him," Charlie said.

Jo and Wyatt approached the back passenger window and looked inside. The guy was handcuffed with his hands behind his back, and kept his eyes toward the floor so Wyatt couldn't get a good look. "It's hard to tell because it was dark, but he is wearing the same clothes as the guy I saw around my truck tonight." Wyatt studied the face for a while before speaking up. "His face looks familiar, but I don't recall his name," Wyatt said, frustrated with his lack of memory.

"That's okay. We'll run his prints through the computer and see what comes up. I've got a gut feeling we find his prints match the ones we found in the abandoned vehicle at Walmart. Hopefully you'll be able to get some rest once we determine if this is the guy that has been causing you so much trouble," Charlie said.

"Rest, what's that?" Jo joked, trying to lighten the mood.

Charlie pulled away and they retreated inside. Wyatt collapsed on the recliner. Jo retrieved the first aid kit, some Tylenol and a glass of water. "Take two of these," Jo commanded as she held the bottle of Tylenol and water out to him. "Hold still while I clean your wound. This might sting a bit," Jo warned.

"Ouch! What are you doing up there? If feels like you are dousing my skull with alcohol."

"I'm sorry, the antiseptic came out faster than I expected." Jo dabbed up the excess and gently placed a clean bandage back over the area. "How's that feel?"

"Other than the fact that my scalp is on fire, it's fine. Thanks." Wyatt said after sounding so harsh.

"You poor thing," Jo made a face like talking to a child. "Did I hurt you?"

"I was just teasing. It really is fine. Thanks for taking care of me," Wyatt said suddenly serious.

"It looks like it is healing nicely. You should be able to go without a bandage in a few days," Jo exclaimed.

There was a slight glow from around the edge of the blinds to indicate another day was starting. "The vet's office will open in a few hours. Why don't you try to get a little rest before we leave to check on Moose?" Jo said.

"What about you? I know you didn't get much sleep before the explosion jarred you awake," Wyatt said.

"I'm too wired and I smell like a fire pit. I'm going to take a hot shower and make some coffee," Jo replied. "Do you sleep better with the TV on or off?" Jo asked.

"Yeah, turn it to the cooking channel. That always puts me to sleep," Wyatt joked.

Jo turned on the TV and adjusted the volume down low in hopes the noise would help him sleep peacefully, with no bad dreams. She watched as Wyatt closed his exhausted eyes. She wished she could take away his pain.

***

Showered and caffeinated once again, Jo went searching for something to make for breakfast. She found a packet of waffle mix and decided what she needed was waffles and ice cream. Her Mom used to make them for her when she was a child, on Sunday mornings, as a treat. While the waffles were still warm, she would plop a large scoop of chocolate ice cream in the center of a square waffle and place another waffle on top, making a waffle ice cream sandwich. Jo would have to hurriedly eat it before the ice cream melted down her arms. She normally ended up with as much ice cream on her face as in her stomach. She smiled as she thought about how nice it was to be so carefree.

"What smells so good this morning?" Wyatt asked as Jo removed the first waffle from the iron.

"Waffles and ice cream. You want one?" Jo asked, pleased with herself for making breakfast.

"What's wrong with syrup?"

"Nothing is wrong with syrup, but you haven't lived until you try ice cream on your waffles." Jo handed Wyatt his waffle sandwich with chocolate ice cream oozing out the sides. "You have to eat if fast, before the ice cream has a chance to melt!" Jo exclaimed.

Wyatt took an enormous bite as melting ice cream ran down his hand.

"Well, what do you think?" Jo asked eagerly.

"You might just have something here," Wyatt said as he took another mouthful.

By the time Wyatt finished his last mouthful of waffle, Jo removed more waffles from the iron. "Are you ready for another one?" Jo asked.

"No, that one is yours," Wyatt said as he licked his sticky fingers and wiped his face clean. He helped himself to coffee, then watched in amazement as Jo managed to quickly cram her waffle, stacked high with ice cream, in her mouth without getting any on her.

"How did you do that without getting ice cream all over you?"

"Plenty of years of practice."

"And how does someone with your small frame and outrageous eating habits manage to stay so thin?" Wyatt asked.

"I have to fuel all this muscle somehow," Jo joked as she bent her right arm to show Wyatt her muscular bulge, if you could call it that.

Wyatt's cell phone rang and he hurried to answer it when he saw it was the vet. "Is Moose all right?" Wyatt asked.

"I thought you would like to hear that Moose did great overnight. He's much more alert and restless this morning."

"I was just on my way to visit with him. Can I bring him home today?"

"I see no reason why not. You're going to have to find a way to limit his activity though. I don't want him opening up his stitches."

"Fantastic!" Wyatt said. "I'll be there in about thirty minutes." He ended the call and relayed the good news to Jo. Then he remembered he no longer had a vehicle. "Oh, I guess I need a ride to the vet. Were you planning to return to work this morning?"

"No, but that does remind me that I better talk to my parents soon, before the town grapevine catches up to them, and they hear about my house being shot up, the explosion, and the resulting fire. My Mom will be over here in a heartbeat trying to persuade me to move back home again if she thinks my home isn't safe or I can't take care of myself."

"You seem to manage quite well on your own," Wyatt added. "And everything that has happened to you has been my fault. So you can blame me and let them know as soon as Moose is well enough to travel, I will be out of your hair."

"What about a vehicle? Do you have enough money saved to buy a new one?" Jo asked.

"Hopefully I can find a junker, that doesn't cost much, and is mechanically sound. Do you know of any for sale around here?"

"None comes to mind." Jo didn't want Wyatt and Moose to leave. She secretly hoped he wouldn't be able to find a used car he could afford, right away. She had gotten used to having them around and didn't like the thought of them leaving. She had to come up with a way to persuade Wyatt to stay. She looked at her cell phone as it started to ring. She mouthed to Wyatt, "It's my Mom." She braced herself as she answered the phone. "Hi Mom! I was just going to call you."

"What is this I hear from Maria about your house almost burning down last night?"

Maria is the town know it all. She somehow always seems to hear what is going on in everyone's lives. "It was just the carport area. Wyatt's truck caught on fire overnight, but the fire department put out the blaze before it had a chance to spread to my house." She left out the part about the grenade being the source of the fire.

"Like I always tell your Dad, you just can't depend on those older vehicles. I know he makes his living on people fixing up older cars, but you never know what could go wrong."

Jo let her mother ramble on and believe she was correct. "Yeah Mom, the wiring or something may have been worn. I got to run." Jo ended the call before her Mom could say another word. "We better stop by my Dad's store on the way to the vet. He'll not be as easy to convince that there is nothing to worry about."

"Could we also stop someplace so I can buy a new pair of jeans? These have seen better days." The knee was ripped on one leg from where Wyatt had leaped into the back yard, and they were covered in soot and grass stains.

"I don't know. I kind of like the homeless look," Jo said in a teasing voice.

"Is that so?" Wyatt grabbed Jo in a bear hug so she couldn't move, pretending to rub his dirty jeans on her clean clothes.

"Hey, no fair! I can't retaliate for fear of hurting your head," Jo said.

Wyatt made Jo lose her balance and they fell to the floor. Jo broke Wyatt's fall and she was pinned underneath him on the floor.

"Get off of me, you big lummox!" Jo yelled as she looked into Wyatt's eyes.

This was the first time she was seeing Wyatt's true self with his guard down. She liked what she saw, and kissed him.

Wyatt didn't resist and kissed Jo back. Before it went too far, Wyatt pulled back and rolled off of Jo. "I better take a shower so we can get to the vet." Wyatt left Jo lying on the floor, speechless.

Chapter 8

The conversation with Jo's Dad didn't go well. "I ran into Charlie at the diner this morning and he informed me that someone has been trying to kill my daughter."

"It's not as bad as it sounds, Dad."

"Oh, really? How is having your house shot up and then Wyatt's truck blown up not as bad as it sounds?"

"Well, when you put it that way," Jo tried to joke. "Did Charlie also tell you he has a suspect in custody?"

"Yes, he said he's waiting on fingerprint analysis to confirm they have the right person. Son, do you have anything you would like to add?" he asked Wyatt.

Wyatt had been standing quietly beside Jo, waiting for an opening to speak. "I'm so sorry, sir. I never meant to put your daughter in any danger. I'm just as eager as you to understand why someone is trying to kill me."

Before Jo's Dad could say another word, Jo spoke up and quickly changed the subject. "Dad, Moose injured his hip and we were just on our way to pick him up from the vet. The vet is waiting for us to arrive, so we have to run."

"We'll continue this conversation later," Jo's Dad said as they rushed out the door.

The veterinary hospital was only about five minutes away. Jo wanted to make sure that Wyatt knew he and Moose were welcome as long as they needed a place to stay. "You know Moose isn't going to be able to travel for a while, so you might as well plan on staying at my house until both of you are healed."

"I really don't have a choice now that my transportation is toast. Do you think Butch could use some help with his handy man business?"

"You remember what the doctor said, you need to give yourself time to heal. Don't even think about trying to go back to work yet. If you push yourself before you're ready, you'll just end up back in the hospital."

"I'm not the type of person that can just sit around all day. Your parents already think I'm mooching off of you. I need to prove to them that I'm not worthless."

"You know that isn't true. In fact, why don't I ask Dad if you can help out part time around his store? You seem to know enough about car repairs to be able to help customers while I deliver parts in the morning. That way Moose can rest at the store while we work. What do you think?"

"I don't want your Dad to think I'm a charity case. Let me find my own job."

"You would be doing us a favor by helping out. Let me run it by Dad tonight and I'll let you know what he says."

Before Wyatt could object, Jo pulled into the animal hospital parking lot. They rushed inside, eager to see Moose. They were escorted to the back where Moose was being housed in a large kennel. He barked at the sight of Wyatt.

"That's my boy! You sound like you are feeling better today." Wyatt kneeled down to Moose's level and gave him a big bear hug to show him how much he was missed.

Moose tried to stand on his three good legs. Wyatt supported him by placing his arms around his middle. That made it easy for Moose to lick Wyatt's face. "I missed you too, buddy. Are you ready to go home?"

The vet went over Moose's care and what to expect from him over the next few weeks. They were handed a list of instructions for cleaning the wound and medicine for pain along with antibiotics to prevent infection. The splint would remain in place for at least six weeks. They were to bring Moose back in a week to make sure the wound was healing properly. Wyatt carried Moose to the truck to protect his injured leg and gently laid him across the seat. He scooted under Moose's large head and stroked it gently.

There was barely enough room left in the front seat for Jo. She didn't mind, though, it felt good having Wyatt and Moose together again and so close.

They arrived home and Moose managed to hobble around on his three good legs. He immediately checked out his food dish to see if there was anything waiting for him.

"That's a good sign," Jo said. "The vet said we could give him small amounts of food."

Wyatt had picked up some canned dog food as a treat for Moose. He dumped a congealed lump of beef flavored dog food into his bowl while Jo filled up his water dish. Moose gulped down the food in two bites and then slurped up his water.

"Well, you didn't waste any time making that disappear," Wyatt said with a smile. Moose looked up from his water dish, drooling water all over the kitchen floor.

"How about swallowing some of that," Jo laughed as she wiped up the puddles with a paper towel. "You've got to be hungry also. How about I fix us one of my famous grilled cheese sandwiches with a bowl of chicken noodle soup?"

"That sounds awesome," Wyatt replied.

"Why don't you place Moose's comforter on the floor in the family room and rest with him while I make us some lunch?"

"I think I can handle that."

Jo walked into the family room with a tray of food. She found Wyatt lying on the floor with his arm over Moose's side. They were both sound asleep. Exhaustion had caught up with him. She set the tray of food down and gently covered him with a blanket. Then she returned to the kitchen, trying to decide what to do with all the food she had made. She ate one of the grilled cheese sandwiches and placed the soup in a storage container to heat up later for Wyatt. The last few days had also caught up with her. She retreated to her bedroom to rest, but first she wanted to talk to Dad.

"Hi, Dad. How are you holding up at work without me?"

"Your cousin has been a big help, but he just isn't as familiar with the inventory as you."

"Well, now that Wyatt's head is healing nicely and Moose is home from the vet, I wanted to let you know I plan to return tomorrow."

"You sound tired. Are you sure you don't need a day to rest?"

"I plan on taking it easy the rest of the day, so I should be as good as new tomorrow," Jo explained.

"You know you can call me or your Mom if you ever need anything. I know you enjoy having your independence, but that doesn't mean you can't come to us for help. I'll think no less of you. You know how proud we both are of you."

"I appreciate that, Dad. I'm really good, though. You don't have anything to worry about. Wyatt is a great guy and is eager to get back to work as soon as he is physically able. I'll see you in the morning," Jo said as she ended the call.

Jo wasn't always the easiest kid to raise. She was a bit headstrong and felt she knew what was best for her by the time she was twelve. That's why it's so difficult for her to share everything going on in her life with her parents. She didn't want to disappoint them. She fell into a deep sleep as exhaustion from the last two days took over. In her dreams she could hear a dog barking. Then she realized it was Moose that she heard, and leaped out of bed to make sure he was all right. Wyatt was having a nightmare and was standing in the family room ready for battle with his gun in his hand.

"Wyatt, wake up! It is just a nightmare," Jo yelled repeatedly as Moose barked loudly.

Wyatt's eyes slowly came into focus and looked down at Moose. Then he saw the gun in his hand, with his arm extended, pointing toward Jo.

Jo, with her hands raised in the air, spoke slowly and calmly. "It's all right, Wyatt. It's just me. You're safe. You can put your gun down."

Wyatt immediately released the weapon and set it on the end table when he realized what he was about to do. He collapsed on the sofa, rubbing his face, trying to remove the vision from his head. "I'm sorry. I was back in Afghanistan. It felt so real," Wyatt said, trying to explain.

"I know. You don't have to justify your actions to me. I still think it's your brain trying to help you remember what led to your accident. Who were you about to shoot in your dream?"

"I was back at the school. The children were playing soccer, like before," He stopped to try to understand what he saw in his head. "I followed someone into a dark hallway. He doesn't know I'm behind him. He's placing something in a room. It's hard to see in the dark. I notice a timer blinking as the seconds count down. I raise my gun to stop the man intent on blowing up the school. The man hears me and looks up. He's staring straight at me. I can't make out the face, though. It's too dark," Wyatt said, frustrated.

Before Jo could ask any more questions her phone rang. "It's Charlie," she shared. "We'll be right there," Jo said into the phone.

"What did he say?" Wyatt asked impatiently.

"He wants us to come down to the station. The guy he picked up, after your truck exploded, wants to talk to you."

"Did he give you a name? Maybe I would recognize him if I had a name."

"No, all he said was the guy requested you specifically. Charlie asked if I would mind bringing you down to the station."

"I don't want to leave Moose alone and I don't think he's well enough to be going all over town with us. Would you stay with him and let me take your truck to the station on my own?" Wyatt asked.

"You're right. I totally forgot about Moose's situation. Yes, of course I'll sit with him while you find out why this guy wants to talk to you. Be careful. He has tried to kill you twice and this may be another ploy to kill you for good."

"What could he possibly do? He's handcuffed in a police station."

"Yeah, I guess you're right. I don't trust him, though. Here are my keys," she tossed them to Wyatt.

"Thanks!" Wyatt took the keys and kissed Moose on top of the head. "You stay with Jo. I'll be right back," Wyatt said before leaving.

Moose tried to get up and follow Wyatt out the door. "It's all right, boy. Wyatt needs to go alone. Take it easy and lay back down," Jo said as she sat beside Moose on the floor, stroking his smooth coat. She thought about what Wyatt's dream could possibly mean. Who is the person that Wyatt's mind is refusing to let him see?

***

Wyatt drove carefully. This was the first time back behind the wheel since he drove to Wheeler several days ago. He pulled into the police parking lot and found a vacant visitor space. He was

72

greeted by Charlie when he entered the building. "Any idea why this guy wants to talk to me?"

"No. So far he refuses to tell us anything. His prints are not in the system, so I have no way of getting his name. I asked him why he tried to kill you and he didn't say a word. I left him alone for a while, hoping maybe he would start talking. Then the only thing he said was he wanted to speak with you."

"That's strange. I don't even know who he is," Wyatt said.

"Maybe if you talk to him he'll tell you why he is trying to kill you and we can figure out who he is," Charlie said.

"Hey, I'm game. Just show me where you're holding him."

"I think we have a better chance of him sharing if I'm not in the room with you. I'll be standing right outside looking through the two way mirror and listening to what he has to say. The first sign of any trouble and I'm coming in," Charlie emphasized.

"Understand. I will remain calm to hopefully keep the situation under control so you don't have to intervene," Wyatt said before entering the interrogation room.

Wyatt took a seat across from the man that he was seeing up close for the first time. He was surprised at his age. He couldn't be more than eighteen years old. Wyatt spoke first. "You seem to know who I am, but I don't believe we have met. My memory isn't that good, though, since my accident. How do you know me?" Wyatt asked.

Angry eyes stared back at him. "We've never met, but my brother talked about you."

"So, I know your brother. Who is he?" Wyatt asked anxiously.

"It's someone you served with."

Then Wyatt suddenly recognized the face from a picture he had seen. "You're Shaun, Rob Manocini's little brother, aren't you? He always carried a photo of you in his pocket for good luck. You were only about thirteen when the picture was taken, that's why I couldn't remember you."

The kid seemed surprised by Wyatt's realization and suddenly became quiet.

"I've been trying to find out about Rob since my injury, but no one will tell me if he survived the explosion. Did he make it out of Afghanistan alive?"

Shaun became very angry and stood up to take a swing at Wyatt.

Charlie stormed into the room and grabbed hold of the suspect and forced him back into his seat. "Sit back down!" Charlie said firmly. "Wyatt deserves an explanation, not your wrath. If you know something, then you need to tell him."

"Rob is dead and you killed him."

Wyatt was left speechless by what he heard.

Charlie spoke up, "What do you mean Wyatt killed him?"

"Wyatt knows what he did. He just didn't think anyone knew," Shaun spoke up.

"I have no idea what you're talking about. I thought I tried to stop Rob from entering the building. But it was too late. The building exploded before I could get to Rob to warn him."

This just enraged him. "You didn't try to save him. You sent him to his death!"

"No, I know that couldn't be how it happened. I don't know who told you this, but Rob was my best friend. I would've given my life to save him."

Now there was no calming Shaun down. He yelled at Wyatt, "I'm going to kill you if it is the last thing I do!"

"Wyatt, you need to leave," Charlie commanded.

Wyatt left the interrogation room shook up by what he had just heard. He couldn't figure out why Shaun would think he killed Rob. He watched Charlie through the two way mirror as he tried to get Shaun back under control.

Charlie strongly encouraged Shaun to calm down. "If you do not control your temper, I'll have to place you somewhere a lot less comfortable."

Shaun sat back down and his beet red face slowly returned to normal.

"This can go one of two ways. I can throw you in a cell with some of our more hardened criminals, or you can start cooperating. It's your choice," Charlie said as he left the room to give the kid a chance to think about his options.

Charlie motioned for Wyatt to follow him. "Come to my office so we can talk in private," Charlie said.

Wyatt took a seat across from Charlie's cluttered desk. "Well, at least we now know the name of who you have in custody. When you told Jo and I the vehicle that followed us was registered to Rob, I should have guessed that it might have been his brother that was driving the car. Shaun can't be any older than eighteen. I remember Rob showing me a photograph of his young brother during one of our boring treks across the desert. The picture was taken when he was only around thirteen. He was dressed in a crisp new blue and white softball uniform. Rob said the photo was taken just before the game. His young brother always looked up to Rob and followed him around, wanting to be included in whatever he was doing. Rob kept the photo as a reminder of what waited for him when he returned home. How could someone Shaun's age have gotten his hands on a grenade? He has to have an accomplice that's filling his head with these lies. There is no way I killed Rob."

"Yeah, I was thinking the same thing." Charlie typed a few key strokes on his computer and clicked his mouse. "There are no guns registered in Shaun's name. It will be difficult to prove he's the one that shot up Jo's house without finding the weapon with his fingerprints on it. The only thing that ties him to being responsible for the shooting or the blowing up of your truck is his fingerprints being in Rob's SUV. You cannot even positively identify him as being the one you saw in your truck with the grenade, because you couldn't see his face in the dark. I really don't have enough evidence to hold him on unless we find a gun," Charlie said.

"Maybe if you let him go he'll lead us to whoever is the real mastermind behind this," Wyatt said.

"That's a possibility, but he may also try to kill you again. You heard that kid. He's convinced you killed his brother and wants nothing more than to see you die. I'm going to hold him for twenty four hours and see if I can get him to give me the name of who he's working with. If I can convince Shaun he's going to jail for a real long time unless he can provide information leading to the arrest of who else is involved, then maybe he'll be more willing to share. In the meantime, you need to watch your back. If he does have an accomplice, then that person is still out there, and wants you dead."

"Yeah, I thought of that also. I just wish I could remember everything that happened leading up to the time of the explosion that landed me in a coma. There has to be an explanation for all this. I just can't believe the only reason this is happening is because Shaun thinks I'm responsible for Rob's death. There has to be more to the story that I can't remember and Shaun isn't sharing." Wyatt slammed his fist against his head in frustration.

"Give it time. Maybe your memory will come back."

"Now you sound like Jo."

"I'll give you a call if Shaun decides to talk."

***

Wyatt entered the house and was greeted by Moose with a bark and a smile from Jo, who was sitting on the floor beside him. Wyatt joined Jo on the floor, giving Moose a big hug to show how much he loved him.

"Well, what did you find out?" Jo asked impatiently.

"The person Charlie arrested is Rob Manocini's baby brother, Shaun. He's under the impression I killed Rob, and is determined to get revenge."

"I thought you said that you thought Rob was killed in the same explosion that injured you?" Jo asked.

"That is what I said. But now I'm starting to think that something else happened to Rob, and someone is trying to blame me."

"If Rob didn't die in the explosion, and was murdered instead, maybe they're trying to put the blame on you to hide their own guilt."

Wyatt tried to remember the days leading up to his injury. "I can remember my unit being sent on a special assignment. It was dark and it took us a while to get into position. We were holed up in an abandoned building, staying low and out of sight. The tension seemed to be growing among us as we waited for whatever lied ahead. Then all I have are flashes of memories of something to do with a tunnel, a schoolyard full of children playing,

76

and the explosion. I don't know if any of it is real, though, or just my mind playing tricks on me," Wyatt said sadly.

"You obviously were involved in something that someone doesn't want you to remember and reveal their secret," Jo stated.

"We have one last hope. If Charlie can get Shaun to talk and tell him who he's working with, then maybe we can get some answers. Until then, though, it's very possible that someone other than Shaun wants me dead. As long as I stay with you your life will be in danger. Moose and I need to find a place to hole up until I can straighten all this out," Wyatt said.

"I can't let you do that. Your head is still healing and Moose needs someone to help take care of him until his hip is better." Jo feared what would happen if they left. She knew Wyatt needed her help, even though he didn't realize it yet. She wished he wasn't so stubborn.

"I have no choice. If I stay, then I will endanger your life. I couldn't live with myself if anything ever happened to you. You have been so kind to Moose and me, but I can't risk putting your life in jeopardy any longer," Wyatt insisted.

"You don't even have a vehicle. How are you going to leave?" Jo asked.

"I have some money saved, and was hoping you could find me a cheap truck or car to buy. Do you think your Dad may know someone that has a vehicle for sale?" Wyatt asked.

"Have you even considered that if this guy is so desperate to hunt you down and kill you, what will stop him from killing me if he thinks I might know where you are located?"

"Yes, I have actually thought about that, and fear your life may be in jeopardy due to   your association with me. But I hoped if I made a big scene leaving the area that whoever is after me would know to leave you alone and follow me instead. Maybe I could set a trap for them."

"I have an idea. My parents bought an RV when I was a kid so we could travel and explore. My Dad and I used to love to go camping together in it. That was kind of our special time together without Mom. We haven't used the RV in a while but I know Dad has kept it operational. We could take it someplace where we couldn't be found to give Charlie a chance to catch who is trying to kill you," Jo said excitedly. "Whether you know it or not you still need me to help with Moose until your head is better. What if you have an episode and no one is there to wake you? You may hurt yourself, or worse, Moose!"

Wyatt paused before speaking. He wanted to believe that he was strong enough to handle whatever came his way, but in actuality, he couldn't trust his own thoughts to know if they were real or not. Also, he hated to admit it, but he had become quite fond of Jo and would worry about her safety if he left.

Jo took Wyatt's hesitation as surrendering to her plan. "Great! It's settled then. I will call Dad and ask to borrow his motorhome. We can pack everything we'll need tonight to hide in the woods until we can come up with a better plan."

A smile crossed Wyatt's face. He loved the way Jo stood up to him and took charge. "I guess there is no point in arguing with you, once you've made up your mind."

Jo already had her cell phone out and was calling her Dad. "Hey, Dad. Do you think you could survive without me for a few more days?" She proceeded to explain everything to him, and by the end of the call had his approval. "Everything is set!" Jo exclaimed.

Wyatt could tell, with her negotiation skills, he was never going to win a fight. Before he could say another word, Jo was planning what they needed to take with them on their trip.

"We will need enough supplies to be able to hide for a few days, at least. The camper is equipped with pots and pans, a small stove and fridge. We will need to make sure the propane tanks are full and fill the water tank before leaving. I'll run to the store and buy some items like bread, peanut butter, pancake mix, cereal, hot dogs, chips, cookies, dried mashed potatoes, aluminum foil, paper towels. Oh, and I can't forget toilet paper. One time Dad and I went camping and we forgot to pack toilet paper. We ended up using leaves, which was just gross! I'll never forget the toilet paper again," Jo laughed.

Wyatt could see how much Jo was loving the chance to go camping again. "I'll pack some stuff for Moose. He'll need his medicine, food, bowls, and comforter to sleep on," Wyatt added. "Do you have some sleeping bags?"

"We won't need them. There is a double size bed in the camper," Jo said. Then, as an afterthought, she realized what Wyatt was probably thinking. "Also, the dining room table makes out into a bed." She didn't want him thinking she was easy and was just going to sleep in the same bed with him. Even though she wouldn't mind, if that is what happened. She smiled to herself.

The rest of the afternoon they both packed for their trip. Wyatt was accustomed to roughing it and didn't need much to be comfortable. Jo, on the other hand, packed everything but the kitchen sink. The living room was full of stuff she couldn't live without.

Wyatt looked over the pile. "We're going camping for just a couple of days, do you really need to take a hair dryer and all of these books?"

"My hair becomes a frizzy mess if I let it air dry, but I guess you're right, I can go a few days without washing it. I thought I might have time to catch up on some reading," Jo added.

"How are we on ammo and weapons? I only have a few clips for my 9 mm. We may want to pick up some more bullets," Wyatt said.

Jo held up her revolver and rifle. "I have plenty of rounds in case we need them."

They waited for dark, then loaded everything in the back of Jo's truck. Wyatt kept a watchful eye to make sure no one was waiting for them outside. Lastly, Wyatt lifted Moose onto the front seat. Jo drove to her parents' and parked in the back yard so her truck couldn't be seen from the street. They transferred everything from the truck to the motorhome.

Jo hugged her Dad and Mom tightly. "Don't worry, with Wyatt's survival skills we'll be fine. I'll contact you when I have a cell signal, to let you know we're safe."

"I don't like this, but I know there is no use in trying to talk you out of it. Take care of my daughter. I just hope they catch this guy soon."

"Don't worry, sir. She's in good hands and I won't let anything happen to her."

Jo climbed into the driver's seat and Wyatt helped Moose into the back. He lifted Moose and placed him on his comforter on the floor. Wyatt sat in the captain's chair next to Jo, to help navigate, and to keep Jo company and make sure she stayed alert.

Jo waved good-bye to her parents as she carefully drove down the driveway. It had been awhile since she last drove the large RV and she didn't want to damage it. She had been running on adrenaline and hoped she could stay awake for a few more hours until they reached their destination. They drove away under the cover of darkness, hopefully hidden from whomever wanted Wyatt dead.

Chapter 9

The drive was uneventful. All they saw were the eyes from a few deer glowing from the headlights as they drove past them along the side of the road. There were only a few cars on the back country roads this late into the night. Jo glanced at the rear view mirror frequently to make sure no one was following them. She slowly wound around the curvy mountain road. Her plan was to stop once they arrived at a small campground where she used to vacation with her Dad while growing up. She looked over her shoulder to check on Moose and Wyatt. Wyatt had converted the dining room table into a bed and was asleep with Moose snuggled up close to him. His headache had persisted after the long, eventful day. Jo finally persuaded him to take some Tylenol and lie down to ease his pain. She was glad to see him resting soundly without any nightmares. She finally arrived at the entrance to the campground and turned onto a gravel road. She drove slowly, bumping along so as not to wake up Wyatt. She was lucky and found a peaceful spot right on the lake to park. It was isolated, with no other campers close by. It was well past midnight, so all the campfires had been put out for the night. This time of year the nights were starting to dip into the 40's, limiting the number of diehard campers to just a handful.

Jo decided to wait until morning to hook up the water and power. Exhaustion had set in and all she wanted to do was crawl into bed and sleep for a week. She quietly got up from the driver's seat and threw an extra quilt over Wyatt and Moose before retreating to the back bedroom. Moose opened his eyes just briefly. After seeing it was just Jo he went back to sleep. She slid underneath the covers and heard an owl hooting in the trees not far away, then another owl responding in the distance. The hooting back and forth continued for a few minutes as the nocturnal birds communicated back and forth, sending her into a deep sleep.

Jo woke with a start, unable to breathe. There was a hand over her mouth. She started thrashing to get away, fearful for her life. She opened her eyes. The attacker was illuminated only by the moonlight seeping through the bedroom windows. Her eyes slowly came into focus. Wyatt was standing over her. He held his finger over his lips signaling for her to be quiet. She shoved Wyatt's hand away from her mouth, furious with him. He had a gun in his right hand and motioned he had heard a noise outside.

"Stay put," Wyatt whispered before quietly exiting the camper.

A deep growl came from Moose, now sitting up alert in bed. Jo wasn't about to stay inside while Wyatt was walking into who knows what. She grabbed her rifle from beside the bed. Before she could get to the door, she heard a loud clatter and then the sound of something running through the brush. She reached for the door, but before she could open it, Wyatt swung the door open and stepped back inside.

"There is nothing to worry about. You can go back to bed," Wyatt said.

"So what was making all that racket?" Jo asked.

"It was just a raccoon searching for food."

"You scared the bygeebies out of me for a raccoon!" Jo said angrily.

"I thought maybe someone had followed us here and was trying to surprise us," Wyatt said in his defense.

"No one followed us. I made sure. Now let's try to go back to sleep. It'll be light in only about an hour and I would like to have one undisturbed night's rest," Jo said, exasperated at Wyatt.

Wyatt looked at Jo with a smile on his face.

"What?" Jo asked.

"I like your Tigger flannel pajama's and wooly socks," Wyatt said jokingly.

Jo couldn't even come up with a response, she was so exasperated with him for scaring her half to death. She stormed back to her bed and climbed under the thick covers to get warm. Jo's adrenaline was off the charts after being awakened by Wyatt with such a start. She stared up at the ceiling of the camper as the glow from the moon penetrated the darkness. She knew there was no more sleep for her tonight. She called out to Wyatt, feeling guilty for being so mad at him, "You asleep?"

"No," Wyatt replied.

"Dad always keeps a stock of movies for us to watch in the bedroom cabinet. Do you want to watch a movie with me?" Jo asked.

"Sure," Wyatt replied.

"Bring Moose in here and place him on my bed so we can keep him company while I go outside and hook up the power," Jo said. She picked up the flashlight on her night stand and walked briskly outside before the cold could creep in. She removed the power cord from storage and plugged it into the electrical box provided at the campsite. She returned, shivering, and pushed Moose over far enough so she could climb underneath the blankets. Moose pressed his warm fur against her side helping to bring her body temperature back up.

"Brrr, it's cold out tonight. Maybe I should turn on the furnace," Jo said.

"I can think of another way to get you warm," Wyatt said.

"I bet you can," Jo said as she rolled her eyes. She turned on the lamp by her bed and grabbed a handful of DVDs. She looked through the discs until she found one she thought they would enjoy. "Have you seen The Ghost and Mr. Chicken with Don Knotts?"

"No, I've never even heard of that movie."

"You'll love it. It's so funny," Jo said as she turned on the television and slid the disc into the DVD player. She pulled the covers up to her chin to get warm. The small bed was barely big enough for two people. Moose moved down to the foot of the bed so he could stretch out, causing Jo to curl up in a ball and lean toward Wyatt to stop from falling off the bed.

"Comfy?" Wyatt asked sarcastically after Jo finally settled down.

"Very, and you?"

"I couldn't be happier."

Jo smiled to herself at Wyatt's response and hated to admit she was happier than she had been in a long time. She snuggled up against Wyatt's muscular shoulder and fell asleep about halfway through the movie.

Wyatt watched her sleep and wished he could stay with Jo forever. He knew his time was limited, though. Once she was out of danger he would have to leave.

Chapter 10

Jo and Wyatt slept in late, with no more disturbances. Jo woke first to find Wyatt's arms wrapped securely around her. Moose had moved to the floor, allowing Wyatt to slide closer. She tried to ease from underneath his arms without waking him.

"Where do you think you're going? Your Tigger pajamas are keeping me warm," Wyatt said as he pulled her closer to him.

"I was just going to make us a late breakfast." Knowing what Wyatt was probably thinking, she added, "Don't even think about having anything other than eggs and bacon for breakfast."

"You're no fun!" Wyatt joked.

Jo slipped into the bathroom and put on a sweat shirt and jeans before Wyatt could change her mind about breakfast. She started a pot of coffee before scrambling a half dozens eggs, frying eight strips of bacon, and popping four buttermilk biscuits in the oven.

Wyatt helped lift Moose off the floor by providing him support so he could stand. Moose was still a little wobbly, learning to walk on three legs. Wyatt coaxed him outside so he could relieve himself. The cool, crisp morning took Wyatt's breath away and quickly had Moose full of energy. The lake was smooth as glass. Wyatt watched as a fish jumped in the distance. It was so peaceful and quiet. He could very easily adapt to roughing it in the camper for a few weeks.

After Moose finished with his business and checked every tree for squirrels, Wyatt returned inside just in time to find Jo placing enough food for an army on the table. "Are we expecting company?"

"No, I'm starving. Did we forget to eat supper last night?"

"Don't you remember running by the burger joint and pigging out on a bacon cheeseburger, fries, and shake last night on the way to your parents?"

"Oh, yeah. It must've been all the excitement with the raccoon last night that has me so hungry," Jo said as she stuffed half a biscuit covered with grape jelly in her mouth.

Wyatt gave Moose a bowl of food before joining Jo at the table. He watched as Moose hungrily gobbled it down until his bowl was licked clean. "Looks like Moose has his appetite back this morning. He must be feeling better." Wyatt took his time enjoying not having to eat alone and savored every bite.

"I thought after breakfast we could take a bike ride down to the country store. We should have cell service there and can check to see if there are any messages from Charlie or my parents."

"You brought bicycles?"

"Dad always kept two folding bicycles in the storage area for us to use when we went camping. Hopefully they are still there and functional. The tires may need some air."

"How far down the road is this country store?"

"It's about three miles. We can pick up some fishing supplies while we're there and try to catch our supper this afternoon."

"You know how to shoot a gun, all about car repairs, camping, can make an awesome breakfast, and now I discover you like to fish, too. What other amazing talents do you have?" Wyatt asked teasingly.

"You'll just have to stick around long enough to find out," Jo said as she cleared the table.

Moose wore out easily, still healing from the loss of blood and surgery. He curled up on his comforter and went back to sleep after breakfast. Wyatt helped Jo remove and assemble the bicycles from the storage area. They were a little dusty, but after putting air in the tires and removing the grime they were good to go. In the daylight, Wyatt surveyed his surroundings. They were parked on a beautiful fifty acre lake with large pine trees towering all around them. There were only a few other campers present. The morning was crisp, but the sun made it feel quit comfortable while peddling to the store.

The country store was an old rustic log cabin that specialized in homemade items. It was still just like Jo remembered from many years ago. She eyed the fresh fried pies made with wild blueberries, peaches, and apples while Wyatt inspected the local honey and jams for sale. There were also all kinds of homemade chocolate, cookies, and candies to choose from, along with camping supplies.

"Can I help you find something?" the older, weathered looking man behind the counter asked.

"Do you have any nightcrawlers for sale?" Jo asked.

"Yes, you can buy one container for three dollars or two for five."

"We'll take two, and hope the fish are biting today," Jo responded.

"Where are you visiting from?"

"We're from Wheeler."

Before Jo could share any more pleasantries, Wyatt spoke up, "We better get going if we're going to catch supper."

Once outside the store Wyatt said, "You need to be careful what you tell people about us. Remember, we are supposed to be hiding from whomever might be after me. What if someone trying to find us just happens to stop by this store and asks about a couple from Wheeler? I'm sure this nice old man wouldn't hesitate to share where we're staying."

"I hadn't thought about that. Surely no one will think to look for us here."

"I hope you're right." Wyatt turned on his cell phone. "I have one bar and a message." He quickly pressed the button to receive his messages and held the phone to his ear to listen.

Jo quickly checked her phone and saw there were no messages. She hurriedly typed a text to her Dad. All safe and sound, and hit send. She turned off her phone so it couldn't be traced. She watched Wyatt's expression as he listened to his voicemail and then ended the call. When Wyatt didn't volunteer any information, she impatiently asked, "Who was it and what did they say?"

"Well, the sheriff got Shaun, Rob's brother to talk."

"Did he reveal the name of the person trying to kill you?"

"Shaun said Carson Marshall approached him after Rob's funeral. He told him how sorry he was for his loss and explained that he had served with Rob. Shaun asked him if he was with Rob when he died and Carson said yes. Carson proceeded to tell Shaun that I killed his brother."

"So do you know this Carson guy?"

"Yes, he was part of our unit, but I wouldn't consider us close. He was pretty much a loner that stayed to himself most of the time. I hardly spoke two words to the guy the entire time we served together. I always felt there was something off about him, though. He rarely showed any emotion, and was almost robotic-like on our missions."

"Can you think of any reason why he would lie and say you killed Rob?"

"You are assuming he was lying. I don't exactly remember how Rob died. I just assumed he was killed in the same explosion that caused my injuries."

"On the day you were injured, do you remember seeing Carson?"

Wyatt struggled to remember. "I'm sure he was part of our convoy, but was probably in a separate Humvee."

"Can you think of any reason he would want you dead?"

"No, like I said, I hardly knew the guy. Oh, and the sheriff said that Shaun confessed to blowing up my truck, but that was it. He said he had nothing to do with shooting me in the head on Old Mill Pond Road or shooting up your house. He heard I was staying at your house and just wanted me to suffer for what I had done to his brother by destroying something precious to me, my truck. When the sheriff asked how he managed to get hold of a hand grenade, he became quiet and wouldn't tell the sheriff."

"I get the feeling Carson is key to what's going on."

"Yeah, the sheriff said his parents live in Idaho and he contacted them, trying to locate Carson. They were not very forthcoming, though. If the sheriff can talk to Carson, he might be able to determine his whereabouts the day I was shot in the head off Old Mill Pond Road, and the night your house was pelted with bullets. Then we can eliminate one more suspect, if he wasn't involved. Charlie said he would keep me posted, but it would probably be best to stay out of sight for now."

"I know what will help to solve this mystery. We need to go fishing, just relax, and enjoy the day. I find when I'm doing something, where I can just clear my mind, is when I find the most clarity in my life."

"When did you become such a philosopher?"

"I just mean, take for instance, mowing the grass. It is a mindless task that allows your mind to wander as you go around and around the yard cutting the grass with each pass. You don't worry about bills or work, you can just relax, and enjoy the moment. That's when I come up with my best ideas or remember something that I was supposed to do. It allows my mind to stop multi-tasking and slow down long enough for me to focus. Hopefully, fishing will help to ease your mind and maybe a memory will creep back in."

With two styrofoam containers filled with worms, and a bag containing two fresh fried apple pies, they made their way back to the campsite. They slowly peddled their bicycles, enjoying the view on the way.

Jo removed the fishing gear and chairs from the storage area while Wyatt stepped inside to check on Moose. He helped Moose clumsily climb down the RV steps so he wouldn't put any weight on his injured leg.

Moose was glad to be free and out in the cool air. After taking in all the new smells, he settled down by lying between Jo's and Wyatt's chairs along the bank of the lake.

It was now after one and the sun was warming them nicely. Jo peeled off her sweatshirt to reveal a t-shirt with a largemouth bass on the front. She handed one of the fishing poles to Wyatt, then dug through the worm container and pulled out a big worm. "You look like you could be a tempting meal for a large bass or catfish." She threaded the worm on the hook and rinsed her hands off in the lake.

Wyatt was entertained, watching how comfortable Jo was handling the stinky, gooey worms. Most women would cringe at the thought of touching a worm. He baited his hook and cast his line in the opposite direction from Jo's. He sat back down in the large, comfortable collapsible fishing chair, enjoying the quiet while he waited for a bite. He was amazed that Jo didn't feel the need to fill the silence with chatter. He couldn't remember the last time he was able to relax and observe the wonders of nature around him. He watched as Canadian geese floated in the water not far from them, looking for food before heading south for the winter.

"Look there," Jo whispered as she pointed to a downed tree in the water about thirty yards away.

A beaver was swimming around the fallen tree. It was bringing in fresh cut branches to reinforce his home. While Wyatt was distracted watching the beaver, his line jerked so hard he almost lost his pole.

"You got a bite!" Jo screamed in excitement.

Wyatt set the line and the drag started going out.

Moose barked with excitement and stood up on his three good legs. He was eager to see what all the noise was about.

"You must have a big one! Don't lose it," Jo instructed.

Wyatt's pole was bent almost in half from the weight of the fish. The fish started to tire after about ten minutes of fighting, and surfaced just long enough for them to get a glimpse.

"Wow, it's enormous!" Jo said. "I'll get the net."

Wyatt slowly wound in the fish, taking his time so the line wouldn't break. When the fish was finally close enough to the shore, Jo kneeled down and scooped it up with the net.

"That's a beauty. It must weigh at least six pounds," Jo said as she placed it in a cooler full of water.

"I caught my supper, now it's your turn," Wyatt teased.

"Yeah, yeah. Just wait and see what I catch next." Jo threw her line back out in the water as far as she could.

Moose laid back down in the cool grass, but stayed alert, watching every movement with anticipation for the next strike.

It wasn't long before Jo's line started to run. She jumped up and set the hook. "I got it!" Jo screamed with excitement as she held on tightly and reeled in her catch.

Wyatt gabbed the net and stood close, in case she needed help. He got underneath the fish and lifted it out of the water. This time it was a striper.

"It's not quite as big as yours, but it will be tasty for supper."

The afternoon couldn't have been more perfect. They had several more bites and forgot about their troubles. By five they were all fished out and starving. Wyatt cleaned the fish then started a campfire. Jo made a batter to dip the fish in and poured a can of pork and beans in a pot. She placed the batter-dipped fish in an iron skillet heated with a little oil, and the pot with the beans, over the open flames.

While the fish sizzled, Wyatt retrieved a couple of beers from the refrigerator. He unscrewed the tops and handed one to Jo. "To a good day of fishing," Wyatt said as he clinked Jo's beer bottle.

"What is it about being in the outdoors that always makes everything taste so much better?" Jo asked as she took a swig of beer.

"Speak for yourself. The food I ate in the outdoors in Afghanistan sure didn't taste better. I was never so glad to get back to the states where the food didn't come in freeze dried packets."

"My outdoor experiences never included a high mountain or desert climate where I had to worry about being killed. Here, try this and tell me I'm not right." Jo handed Wyatt a plate full of fried fish fillets, baked beans, and some potato chips.

Wyatt took several bites of fish and a large spoonful of beans. "You might be right," he said as he continued to devour the mound of food on his plate.

As they enjoyed their fried apple pies for dessert, Jo spoke up, "I had a thought while we were fishing today. If we could track down someone in your unit, maybe they could help fill in the blanks for the day you were injured. Do you remember if there was anyone that served with you, who was near the end of their tour, that might be state side?"

"I don't really want to drag anyone else into my mess. I figure they probably have enough problems of their own to deal with after returning from Afghanistan."

"I understand your hesitation, but it might be the only way we find out what really happened that day."

After some time, Wyatt said, "There was one guy, Jeff Armer. He was counting the days until he returned home. But I have no idea where he lives or how to get in contact with him."

"Let me worry about that. After supper let's take a drive into town and see if we can find a Wi-fi signal. I bet we can narrow down our search enough to come up with a phone number or address."

Jo drove the RV to a McDonalds about forty five minutes away and sat in the parking lot while she googled Jeff Armer's name. Luckily, only about twenty five came up. "Help me look through this list and see if you recognize your Jeff."

"I'm pretty sure he lived somewhere in the east, near mountains. He talked about fishing for trout in the clear mountain streams. He may have mentioned something about North Carolina, but I can't be sure."

"There are three with a North Carolina address." Jo clicked the first link and came up with an address, but no phone number. The second link had a phone number but the guy was a real estate agent.

"Jeff definitely isn't a real estate agent."

"Okay then, that leaves us with this Jeff who lives outside Murphy, North Carolina. That is only about three hours away. What do you think about a road trip tomorrow?"

"What are we going to do? Walk up to the house and ask if a Jeff Armers lives there, did he happen to serve in the military, and know anyone by the name of Wyatt Deckster?"

"Yeah, what do we have to lose?"

Jo drove back to their secluded spot on the lake and hooked the RV back up to power and water. After a day of fishing everyone was exhausted.

"First dibs on the shower!" Jo yelled.

"Just save me some hot water."

Jo hurriedly cleaned off the grime from the day, scrubbing her fingernails trying to get the worm smell off of them, to no avail. She stepped out wearing sweat pants and a large t-shirt, drying her hair with a towel. "Your turn. I think I left you a little warm water," she teased.

Wyatt resisted the urge to kiss her. He gathered up a dry towel and some clean clothes before stepping in the shower. By the time he was cleaned and dressed, Jo was in bed curled up under her thick blankets, sound asleep. Wyatt looked over at Moose laying on his comforter on the floor. "I guess it's just you and me tonight, boy."

Chapter 11

Jo woke the next morning rested and full of energy. She was ready for whatever the day would bring. "Good morning!" she exclaimed to Wyatt and Moose as she walked by them on the way to the kitchen.

"You're awful cheery this morning," Wyatt said as he slowly crawled out of bed and waited for the coffee to stop dripping.

"There is something about sleeping in the outdoors that is so refreshing. Don't you think?"

"No, I slept in the outdoors enough in Afghanistan to last me a lifetime."

"I hadn't thought about that, but surely these accommodations and the scenery are much better." Jo looked at Wyatt's makeshift bed, converted from the dining room table, and realized he was probably not very comfortable. It was too short for him and his legs hung over the end. It was rather narrow, and with Moose taking up most of the bed, that left only a sliver of space for him.

"Well, at least the only threat to my life has been from a raccoon, and yes, the scenery is much better." Wyatt stared at Jo, making her feel uneasy.

Moose barked to remind Wyatt that he needed to go out. "Okay boy, let's go," he said as he held up his leash.

It wasn't long before Moose came barreling back inside, looking at his empty food dish. Wyatt placed a large scoop of food in the bowl and filled his water dish.

"He seems to be feeling good again today. You didn't even have to help him up the stairs," Jo said.

"Yeah, he is getting good at getting around on three legs. It's good to see him returning back to his old self. Hopefully that means his leg is healing."

"I thought after breakfast we would head to Jeff's house. Does that sound all right with you?"

"I guess its worth a shot. Maybe he can provide me with some answers to what happened the day I was injured."

93

"Also, seeing someone from your unit might help you recall the events of that night."

"I hope you're right. I really don't want to put any of the guys I served with in jeopardy. I need to make sure no one is following us, so plan on making a few stops. I want to survey around to make sure I don't see the same vehicle more than once."

Wyatt helped Jo pack up the chairs and fishing poles. Jo disconnected the power and water and looked around outside the RV to make sure she didn't forget anything. She noticed the antenna was still extended. "Can you lower the antenna for me?" Jo called out to Wyatt. She watched to make sure it was completely down before climbing in the driver's seat to get on their way.

"We'll have to come back here again when we have more time and don't have to worry about anyone finding us," Wyatt said as Jo pulled away from the campsite.

"Yes, this place is definitely a hidden jewel that many people don't know about." She was thrilled to hear that Wyatt thought he might be sticking around long enough for them to go camping together again.

They bounced along the gravel drive until they returned to the main road. Jo looked down at Moose, sound asleep between their seats. "He doesn't seem to be too upset about us leaving," Jo joked.

"Unfortunately, Moose is used to not staying in one place for very long," Wyatt said sadly.

"We might have to see what we can do about that once all this is over. You know you are more than welcome to stay in my guest room as long as you need. I've kind of gotten used to having you around."

That sounded so good to Wyatt, but he didn't dare hope for a life with Jo. He had to be realistic. If Jo knew what he was really like, she'd run away from him in a heartbeat. "There is still a lot you don't know about me. You may regret that offer."

"What's there to know? You love dogs and the outdoors. You are good with a gun and a fishing pole. You like old trucks and are a good listener. What more could a woman want?"

"I'm glad you're so easy to please," Wyatt laughed.

The rest of the trip was uneventful. Jo stopped for gas and lunch. Wyatt searched their surroundings and didn't see anyone suspicious at either stop. As they got closer to their destination, the anxiety in the RV grew. Wyatt worried about Jeff not recognizing him or refusing to talk to him.

As if Jo knew what Wyatt was thinking, Jo said, "Don't worry if this doesn't pan out, we will look elsewhere for some answers."

Jo stopped the RV in front of a single wide mobile home. "Well, this is the address."

"I think it might be best if I go up alone. If this is the Jeff that served with me, he may feel more comfortable talking to me alone."

"I understand. I will wait here and keep Moose company. Just be careful. He may also want you dead."

Wyatt climbed out of the RV and cautiously approached before knocking on the door. He waited, but there was no answer. He was just about to give up when he heard a bandsaw running. He walked around the back of the home and noticed a large shed, with double doors standing open. Jeff was busy cutting some lumber on the saw and didn't notice Wyatt walk up. He didn't want to startle Jeff, and hung back until the saw blade stopped and quiet returned.

"Hey Jeff! I hope I'm not disturbing you?" Wyatt yelled as the saw wound down.

Jeff looked up from his project. "Wyatt, is that you?"

"Yes, you remember me."

"The last time I saw you, you were being loaded into a helicopter on a stretcher. I wasn't sure you were going to survive. What are you doing in my neck of the woods?"

"I was hoping you could help me fill in some blanks in my memory. I'm having trouble remembering the details of the day I was injured."

Jeff's expression changed from friendly to serious. "It's probably best you don't remember."

"Someone is trying to kill me and I think it has something to do with that day. No matter how bad it is, I need to know what happened."

Jeff could see the desperation in Wyatt's eyes. "I can only tell you what I saw, and that may not provide you with the answers you are looking for."

"I understand. Anything at this point would be appreciated."

"What is the last thing you remember?"

"We were on a nighttime mission to check out a location where the Taliban were thought to be hiding. We stopped our Humvees along a ridge and hiked the rest of the way to the compound. That's where my memory starts to fade."

"We reached the compound and it was eerily quiet. It was almost like they were expecting us. The building was deserted and we found no evidence of any Taliban. We regrouped outside and that's when the team noticed you and Rob were missing. About that time we heard a gunshot come from the direction of the school just down the road. We took cover behind a stone wall and listened for any more shots. It was quiet. The team slowly approached the school. Just before we reached the entrance you came stumbling out the door carrying Rob. Before we could signal to you there was a loud explosion. You were thrown through the air and landed motionless. Screams could be heard all around us. We knew we had to get you and Rob out of there before being overrun with Taliban. I ran toward the school and found Rob's lifeless body on the ground not far from you. I lifted him on my shoulders while the other guys checked on you. They created a makeshift gurney and had you secured on it within a minute. People were coming from all directions now with their guns drawn, so time was of the essence. Dodging bullets, we raced back up the ridge to where our vehicles were hidden. Once we got a safe distance away, a helicopter picked you up."

Wyatt stayed silent to see if Jeff added any more information, and when he didn't Wyatt spoke up. "I get the feeling there is more that you're hesitant to share."

"The next day, after we arrived back at camp, rumors starting flying about what had happened inside the school. Supposedly Rob was killed with your weapon. There was speculation that maybe he came up on you by surprise and you shot him."

Wyatt was speechless. Was it true? Could he have killed Rob? He pressed his hands against his head, trying to remember. "That just can't be true. Rob was like a brother to me. There has to be another explanation."

"Like I said, I can only tell you what I saw and heard."

"Do you remember seeing Carson that night?"

"Yes, he was with the group when we searched the building and found nothing. Why do you ask?"

"It's not important. I'm just trying to put all the pieces together from that night."

"No one really knows what happened inside that school but you."

"Someone must know and doesn't want me to find out. Why else are they trying to kill me?"

"I don't know, but I wish you luck finding the truth."

"It looks like you have found some peace after the middle east." Wyatt knew how difficult it was to return to normalcy after what they had seen.

"Yeah, I do all right for myself. I discovered I like working with my hands, and making furniture just seems to come naturally. It's quiet out here and there is no pressure being my own boss. I have a booth at the local flea market where I sell my creations on the weekend."

"I'll have to check it out some time. Thanks for the information. You've helped me more than you realize."

"No problem. Feel free to stop by for a beer anytime, if you want to talk again."

Wyatt returned to the RV and was greeted by a very happy lick from Moose. Wyatt returned his affection with a full body rub. "I missed you, too. Don't worry, I'm not going to leave you again."

Jo couldn't stand waiting any longer to hear what Jeff had told Wyatt. "So what did he say? Was he able to tell you what happened?"

"Yes and no. He was able to confirm that Rob and I got separated from the group and that we were found at the school located next door. But he doesn't know what happened inside the school to cause the explosion, or Rob's death." Wyatt left out, on purpose, the piece of information that Jeff shared about the rumor that a bullet from his gun was responsible for Rob's death.

"Well, that's something. It provides a few more pieces to the puzzle, and might help your memory return. I was thinking while you were talking to Jeff that maybe we're going about this all wrong."

"What do you mean?"

"Instead of hiding from your pursuer, looking for answers, maybe we should make ourselves targets to draw him out."

"I'm not sure that is such a great idea. I couldn't live with myself if you were killed."

"Hear me out. Let's say we return to Wheeler and make ourselves very visible, so whoever is looking for you knows we are back in town. We go home, turn on the television and lights to make it look like we're in the house. Then sneak out the back door and hide where we can't be seen, but someplace where we can watch the house. The sheriff can have his men stake out my house and wait to see if anyone takes the bait."

"I guess that makes more sense than hiding and not getting any closer to finding who is doing this."

"Good, if we leave right now we should be back to Wheeler by six tonight. We can stop by the diner and get supper, to make ourselves seen around town, then visit with the sheriff to get him on board with our plan."

On the ride back to Wheeler, they finalized their plans for making themselves a decoy without getting killed in the process. Now all they needed was for the killer to still be in town waiting for them to return.

***

The sheriff had nothing new to report other than he confirmed Carson was currently on leave from the military. He was still the only suspect of interest that the sheriff was trying to locate.

Jo drove the RV back to her parents' house after they made a noticeable appearance in town. She kept an eye on the rear view mirror, hoping to see someone following them. She pulled into her parents' driveway around seven. After a round of hugs and kisses from her Mom, Jo assured her parents she was no worse for wear than from the last time they had seen each other two days ago.

"Mom, do you still have those sewing dummies you used to make me clothes when I was little?"

"Yes, I think they are buried in the basement somewhere."

"Can I borrow them for a little while?"

"Sure, honey. Are you thinking about trying to sew?"

Jo's Mom tried to teach Jo her homemaking skills when she was growing up, to no avail. Jo had little interest in learning to sew or cook. She would rather spend time with her Dad working on whatever car project he had at the time. "No, I just need them as models for something Wyatt and I are working on."

"If you can find them in that dusty basement, you are welcome to use them."

Wyatt followed Jo into the basement. "What are you scheming now?"

"We need to make it look like we're home. We can dress the dummies up with our clothes and place them in bed or on the sofa so if someone looks through the window they will see us. Here they are!" Jo exclaimed.

Wyatt looked at the full length stuffed dolls, "It's going to take a lot to make that look like me."

"Trust me. A little stuffing to make the clothes fit, glue on a little hair, and place a cover over the body. No one will be able to tell the difference."

They returned upstairs to find Jo's Mom cooking supper. "Can you stay for supper tonight?"

"No, we already grabbed a bite at the diner. Can we take a rain check? Dad, I have one more favor to ask you. Can you watch Moose for us tonight? Wyatt and I are going to be busy and don't want Moose overdoing it with his injured leg."

"Of course. I would be thrilled to spend some time with Moose. I've missed having him at the store with me the last few days."

"Great! I'll call you tomorrow morning and let you know when we can pick him up."

Wyatt removed Moose's belongings from the RV and was shown a place to set them in the family room. He placed Moose's comforter on the floor. "Here, boy," Wyatt patted his hand against the floor to show Moose where he wanted him to lie down. Moose turned around in circles until he felt comfortable, than settled down on his blanket. "Good boy," Wyatt said as he patted Moose's head. "I have to leave you just for the night, but will be back tomorrow. I promise," he said as if Moose could understand every word. Wyatt stood up. "Stay," he commanded as he met Jo outside.

They hurriedly placed the leftover food and supplies from the RV into Jo's truck. Then they headed to Jo's house to set their plan in place.

***

It was already way past dark by the time they arrived home, which helped conceal them from whoever may be watching. They hurriedly staged the house so anyone driving by would see they were home. Jo turned on the television and set the timer on the remote to shut it off at eleven. She did the same with the lights so they would automatically turn off. She placed one of the sewing dummies, now made up to look like Wyatt, under the afghan on the sofa, and the other one in her bed. Jo placed her cell phone on the night stand and Wyatt placed his on the end table in case they were being tracked. They each grabbed a gun and hid it under their coats as they exited through the basement door. They ran the short distance to the woods that surrounded Jo's property. They found a place far enough away from the house where they couldn't be seen, but close enough so they could watch if anyone approached.

"Now we wait," Wyatt said.

"I stuffed a bag of chips and two bottles of water in my jacket in case you get hungry or thirsty." Jo said.

"You're always thinking about food, aren't you?"

"I can't tell. Is that a good thing or a bad thing?" Jo asked.

"Good thing," Wyatt said as he grabbed Jo's hand.

They made themselves comfortable on a fallen log and sat in silence, staring at the house. The lights and television turned off as planned at eleven o'clock.

"If anyone was watching they should be making their move soon," Wyatt said.

Wyatt heard the crinkling of the potato chip bag.

100

"You're going to give us away with all that noise," Wyatt whispered.

"I guess I should have brought a quieter snack. I get the munchies when I'm under duress."

Wyatt wrapped his arms around Jo and held her tightly. Then they heard a car approaching. They watched as it drove slowly by the house.

"Do you think that's the sheriff?" Jo whispered.

"No. He said he was going to park out of sight and watch the house from a distance, like us."

The vehicle drove out of sight, but returned a short time later, driving by in the opposite direction.

"That has to be someone scoping out my house," Jo said. "We never get this much traffic on the road this late at night."

They listened intently as the engine noise faded, but then they heard the car stop with its' engine idling for a few minutes, as if trying to decide what to do. The engine noise stopped.

"They must be getting out of their car," Jo whispered.

They watched as two men approached the house. The men tried the front door, and after determining it was locked, shined a flashlight into the front window. Then they made their way around the back of the house. They picked the lock to gain access.

"You stay here and cover me in case I need help," Wyatt instructed as he got up from their hiding place.

"I thought we were going to let the sheriff handle it?" Jo said.

"I don't want to take a chance that they'll get away. Now stay put and let me do what I've been trained to do."

Jo watched as Wyatt crouched down, staying out of sight in the shadows, making his way silently back to the house. Charlie approached from his hidden vehicle and they both reached the front of the house at the same time, with their weapons drawn. That was when the men inside the house discovered they had been conned. They came racing out the front door, their guns by their sides. Wyatt and Charlie greeted them with their weapons drawn, pointed directly at the men's chests, before the crooks could fire off a shot.

"Don't move or it will be the last thing you ever do!" Charlie said. "Now slowly drop your weapons on the ground."

101

The men complied.

"Turn around and place your hands against the house," Charlie ordered.

The sheriff proceeded to frisk them while Wyatt covered him. He found extra clips for their guns stuck in their belts along with hunting knives. "It doesn't look like you guys were planning a friendly visit tonight." The sheriff cuffed the men and turned them around.

"Do you recognize either of these guys?" the sheriff asked as he shined his flashlight in their faces.

Wyatt studied them, looking directly in their eyes. He wanted them to know he had no intention of backing down. "No, I'm afraid they don't look familiar to me."

Jo came racing out of the shadows and stopped by Wyatt's side, out of breath. "Good job!"

The sheriff searched for IDs, but came up empty. "Would you like to share with me what you were planning to do here? It's obvious you had no intention of robbing the place."

Neither guy said a word.

"Maybe a night in the county jail will help jar your memory. You are being arrested on a breaking and entering with a deadly weapon charge for now." He read them their rights as he escorted them to his police cruiser.

Once the men were secured in the back seat, Charlie turned toward Jo and Wyatt, "I don't like this one bit. No ID, and plenty of ammo, only means one thing. They were planning to kill you and if they got killed or caught in the process, they didn't want anyone to know who they were."

"I know, my thoughts exactly," Wyatt said. "What bothers me even more is that I don't recognize them. I still don't have a clue as to why someone wants me dead."

"If they don't talk, hopefully their prints are in the system and we can get some answers that way. Also, I'll check with ballistics to see if the bullets from either of their guns match the bullets removed from Jo's house. There is nothing more we can do tonight. You guys try to get some rest. I will let you know what I find out tomorrow."

Jo and Wyatt retreated inside. "I don't know about you, but I feel like I'm crawling with bugs after hiding in the woods. I'm going to jump in the shower," Jo said.

"You want some company?" Wyatt teasingly asked.

"Very funny."

"Can't blame a guy for trying," he laughed.

By the time Jo felt clean and bug free, Wyatt was out cold in the recliner. She was still too wound up to sleep. She crawled in bed and pulled out her laptop. She typed in Wyatt's name to see what came up. She found a newspaper article from his younger days that mentioned he was the athlete of the month from an eastern Kentucky high school. "Hmm Wyatt never mentioned he played football," Jo said to herself. She studied his photograph of a younger, but just as lean, and chiseled face. He was probably Mr. Popularity and sought after by all the cheerleaders with his looks, she thought. Next she searched the family services website for any information on his foster families or parents. She found some interesting documents that listed Wyatt's mother's name as Lidi. "That's an unusual name."

While she took in what she had discovered about Wyatt, she decided to see what, if any, information she could dig up on Carson. The sheriff had said his parents lived in Idaho. How many Carson Marshalls could be from Idaho? She found a newspaper article announcing him being accepted into the military. Interesting, the article describes Carson as hard working, smart and very athletic, playing on his high school football team for three years. His parents were mentioned, Ellen and Dale Marshall. Jo googled Ellen and Dale Marshall and found a court record showing the day Carson was adopted by them when he was three years old. She did a double take at the signatures on the adoption paperwork. Carson's biological mother's name is Lidi. That can't be a coincidence. Could Carson and Wyatt be brothers and not even know it?

***

"Get down!" Wyatt yelled.

Jo jumped out of bed and raced into the family room where Wyatt was sleeping in the recliner. "Wake up, you're having another nightmare!" Jo screamed. She tried to shake him awake, but he grabbed her wrist before she realized what was happening.

"Wyatt, it's Jo! Wake up, you're hurting me!" she yelled as she tried to get away.

Wyatt's eyes opened. He stared straight at her but didn't seem to see her. He grabbed her by the neck and started to squeeze.

Jo kicked and flailed with all her might, trying to wake Wyatt from his trance. Her foot came in contact with his groin.

Wyatt released his grip from Jo's neck and bent over in agony.

Jo gasped for air and stepped away from Wyatt.

Wyatt slowly came around. "Why did you kick me?"

"You were having another nightmare. I couldn't get you to wake up."

Wyatt could see the fear in Jo's eyes. "Did I hurt you?"

"No, I'm fine." Jo lied, regaining her composure. She knew Wyatt would be devastated if he found out that he had almost strangled her to death.

Wyatt rubbed his head. "I was back at the schoolhouse."

"Did you remember anything?"

"Someone attacked me from behind. I was trying to fight them off."

"Could you see who it was, or anything around you?"

"No, it was dark. It's always dark in my dreams." Wyatt looked at Jo to make sure she was truly unhurt. "You're dressed in your sweats. Have you even gone to bed yet?"

"Yes, but I couldn't sleep. I was wide awake after catching those two guys who invaded my house, so I did some research online. You might be interested in what I found. Was your mother's name Lidi?"

"Yes, that's what I was told, but I've never tried to find her. Why do you ask?"

"I found some information about Carson. Did you know he was given up for adoption by his mother?"

"No, like I said, I hardly said two words to the guy."

"I want to show you the adoption paperwork."

"Okay. I'm not sure what that will prove."

Jo held her laptop up so Wyatt could see the adoption form.

"So what am I looking for? It says he was adopted by Ellen and Dale Marshall."

"Keep reading. Look at the name of his biological mother."

Wyatt grabbed the laptop to look closer at the signature. "There's no way we have the same mother. This has to be a mistake."

"Carson's birthdate indicates he's three years younger than you. Do you remember if your mother was pregnant when you were three?"

Wyatt rolled his eyes. "Can you honestly remember anything from when you were three years old?"

"Yeah, I guess you're right. You would've been too young to remember. But if your mother did get pregnant again after having you, it's possible she gave that kid up for adoption. She already had one child she couldn't raise and I'm sure she realized it would be for the best."

"That would mean that Carson could be my brother."

"Yes, my point exactly."

"Do you think he knows I'm his brother?"

"Unlikely, since you live so far apart."

"So where does that leave us?" Wyatt asked.

"I think we need to find Carson and ask him why he told Shaun that you shot Rob."

"That's a great plan, but we don't know where Carson is located."

"But we do know where his parents live." Jo turned her computer around so Wyatt could see the address.

"You really want to drive all the way to Idaho on the chance that we might find Carson?"

"It's better than sitting around here and having someone use us for target practice. It's only three hours until the sun comes up and I need some sleep. Then I'll contact Burt at his garage, and ask if he has a car we can borrow. We can pack a few clothes, pick up some road food, some cash so no one can trace our transactions, and retrieve Moose from my parents. Then we should be able to be on our way by lunch. With any luck, we should arrive in Idaho by midnight."

"I get exhausted just listening to you talk. You make it sound so easy. At this point I'm willing to try anything to get some answers. So I'm game."

"Great! Now I need to rest. In a few hours we have a long road trip ahead of us. Who knows, maybe in two days you'll have the answers you've been looking for."

"Always the optimist," Wyatt said with a smile.

Chapter 12

Jo woke to the smell of eggs and bacon. She dragged herself out of bed and followed the tantalizing smell into the kitchen.

"I figured the aroma of food would get you up," Wyatt said.

"What time is it?"

"It's 7:30. I know you've only had a few of hours of sleep, but if we're going to make it to Idaho by midnight, we've got to get moving."

"Yes, I completely agree. Thanks for waking me up." Jo sat at the kitchen table, still half asleep. Her curly hair was sticking up in every direction, looking quite scary. Jo blew the hair from her eyes and slowly came to life.

Wyatt handed her a large mug of coffee. "Looks like you could use this. I brewed it strong."

"Oh, you're wonderful. Will you marry me?" Jo said with a smile across her face.

"If I'd known fixing you breakfast would win your heart, I would've done it days ago."

Jo took a big forkful of eggs, then placed an entire piece of bacon in her mouth, then washed it down with a big gulp of coffee.

Wyatt watched Jo eat in amazement. "I've never seen one person put so much food in their mouth at one time."

"Oh, sorry. I'm starving. I guess it's from all the excitement last night."

Wyatt enjoyed making breakfast for Jo. With her love of food, he was surprised she didn't weigh three hundred pounds. There was never a dull moment with her and he enjoyed all the unexpected surprises. He thought he had everything he needed in life and never felt alone with Moose to keep him company, but he was wrong.

By the end of breakfast Jo was the energizer bunny again, raring to go. "Let me just brush my teeth, try to tame my hair, throw some clothes in a bag, make some peanut butter and jelly sandwiches for the road, and we should be good to go."

"Sounds like you've got everything under control. I'll gather up my things and throw them in your truck."

Within fifteen minutes the truck was packed and they were headed toward Jo's parents' house to pick up Moose.

"I haven't quite figured out what I'm going to tell my parents. I know my Dad is expecting me to return to work someday soon."

"I never meant to take up all your time. Your parents are never going to forgive me if anything happens to you."

"I'll just tell them that I'm going to drive you to meet someone you served with in the military, and that you're going to stay with him until all this can be sorted out. I plan to return in a few days. That's not too much of a lie, is it?"

"I would feel better if we just told them the truth."

"Then they'll just worry themselves to death and I don't want them to be concerned about me." Jo pulled into her parents' driveway and got out before Wyatt could protest. She walked into the house and found her parents still sitting at the table in the kitchen eating breakfast. Moose about knocked Wyatt down, he was so excited to see him.

"Was Moose any trouble last night?" Jo asked.

"No, your Dad made sure he didn't get lonely and let him sleep in our bed."

"It sounds like you were spoiled rotten while I was gone," Wyatt said as he roughed Moose up by rubbing him all over. "How's your leg doing, buddy?"

"He has been running around on three legs, not the least bit fazed with the splint on his right hind leg," Jo's Dad shared.

"Good to hear. That must mean he's not in any pain," Wyatt said as he hugged Moose.

"How did everything go last night?" Jo's Dad asked.

"Good, the sheriff arrested two men found wandering around my house. Hopefully we'll not have any more trouble. Do you think you can survive without me for a few more days? I would like to take Wyatt to visit a guy he served with in Afghanistan to see if he can fill in some more holes to his memory. I should only be gone a few days. Then I promise I'll return to work to help you out."

"Where is this friend of Wyatt's located?"

108

Jo hesitated before telling them the truth. "Idaho. If we leave right now we should be able to make it by midnight."

"That is an awful long drive for you to make. Can't Wyatt just fly there?" her Mom asked.

"We'll take turns driving. It'll be like a mini vacation after everything I've been through lately."

"I know once your mind is made up there is no changing it." Jo's Dad turned his attention toward Wyatt. "If you let anything happen to my daughter, I will haunt you for the rest of your days."

"Understand, sir. I'll keep her safe."

They made a quick exit before her parents changed their minds. Next, Jo drove to Burt's garage to see if he had anything on his lot that she could borrow, and would be a more suitable travel vehicle.

"Hi Burt! How's business?"

"It's been busy and I've missed you delivering my parts."

"I'll be back in the part delivery business very soon, but first I need to ask you for a favor. Do you have a spare vehicle on your lot that you wouldn't mind lending me for a few days? Wyatt and I need to visit a military friend of his in Idaho and my truck will kill my budget on fuel alone."

"I have a vehicle, but it's probably not what you are use to parading around town in."

"It can't be that bad."

They followed Burt to the lot behind his shop. "I just finished repairing this minivan and was going to put it up for sale. You can test drive it for me to make sure I worked out all the bugs."

Jo looked inside. It wasn't bad. It had kind of a funky smell, but a little air freshener would take care of that. It had blue vinyl seats, rubber floor mats and a radio that worked. There was no cruise control, but she could live without that. "This'll work just fine. There's plenty of room for Moose to lie down in the back. I'll leave my truck here with you and be back in a few days."

Burt handed Jo the keys, and after transferring their travel gear, they were on their way to hopefully getting some answers.

109

They arrived in Idaho just before midnight and found a dog friendly motel for the night. Wyatt opened the door to their modestly furnished room. It included two double beds, a television placed at the foot of the beds, and one night stand between the beds.

"I'll take the bed closest to the door," Wyatt said.

"Why, both beds are the same?"

"I like to be nearest to an exit, just in case."

"Just in case what? So you can escape and leave me for dead?"

"No, that's not it at all. I just feel safer when I'm in control. This way I can stop whomever may enter before they have a chance to get to you."

"Ah, how sweet. You don't think I can protect myself?"

"You're impossible. I'm sleeping with my gun under my pillow in case you get any ideas about joining me," Wyatt said with a wicked smile.

Jo threw a pillow at him. "I'm so exhausted, once my head hits the pillow I'm not planning to move until I absolutely have to."

"Have it your way. Moose, it looks like half the bed is yours tonight." Wyatt gently lifted Moose up on the bed so as not to put any pressure on his injured leg. He was fearful of falling asleep and returning to his recurring nightmare. He found a television show on restoring cars and watched it to keep his mind occupied. He turned the volume down low so as not to disturb Jo.

Around six they were both woken suddenly by the sound of someone's car alarm going off. Wyatt peered outside. "I don't see anything suspicious."

"You know how sensitive those alarms can be. It's probably nothing," Jo said as she rolled back over and went back to sleep.

Wyatt had fallen asleep with the television on. He glanced at the screen now playing a show on renovating homes. The wailing alarm outside their room had stopped. He felt restless, wondering what the day would bring, and quietly got up to take Moose for a short walk. The sun was just starting to crest over the horizon. The small town was slowly starting to come to life. He noticed the open sign on the diner across the street. Some coffee sounded good, so he entered with Moose in tow.

"Is it all right if I bring my dog inside with me?" he asked.

The lady behind the counter smiled. "As long as you don't tell the health department. What can I get you?"

"Just some coffee for now."

She placed a coffee cup, filled to the brim with black coffee, in front of him. "Any cream or sugar?"

"No, black is fine."

"Are you traveling through town or here on vacation?"

Wyatt studied the homely looking woman, who appeared to be in her fifties, with Margery on her name tag. He decided it would be safe to share why he was here. "I'm hoping to locate someone I served with in the military. His parents are supposed to live nearby. Do you know a Dale and Ellen Marshall, by any chance?"

"You must be looking for their son Carson."

"Yes, you know them?" Wyatt asked eagerly.

"They have a ranch just outside of town."

Before Wyatt could ask another question, the bell over the door jingled, "There you are! You scared me half to death. I woke and saw you were gone. I was worried something had happened during the night."

"I'm sorry. I knew how exhausted you were and didn't want to wake you. Margery was just telling me that Dale and Ellen Marshall own a ranch just outside of town."

"Great! Let's get some breakfast so we can find Carson."

Wyatt wasn't very hungry. His thoughts were on what they may discover once they found Carson. He picked at two eggs cooked over easy with a piece of toast, and gave half his order to Moose.

Jo, on the other hand, ordered a large stack of pancakes. She drowned them in syrup and butter. She savored every bite.

"You are definitely a woman that enjoys her food," Wyatt said as she licked the syrup from her fingers.

"I don't get to eat like this often. It's normally a pop tart in the truck as I race to work."

"If you decide to keep me around, I'll show you how good eating healthy can taste. When I worked for Mr. Davis he would invite me over for a late night supper after closing the pizza parlor. He was quite a chef, even though he mainly made pizzas for a living. He taught me a lot about cooking healthy meals. You should have tasted his baked chicken that would melt in your mouth or his grilled salmon with vegetables. After the military and hospital food, I thought I had died and gone to heaven, it tasted so good."

Jo thought of how nice it would be to come home after work and spend every evening with Wyatt, eating whatever concoction he came up with. "If you bribe me with food you'll never be able to get rid of me," Jo joked as she crammed the last bite of pancakes in her mouth.

"If you can still move after eating all of that, we need to be on our way."

They checked out of the motel, not sure where they would be staying that night. Margery had been very helpful and provided them directions to the Marshall's ranch. They followed the route outside of town, taking several turns before coming to a stop in front of a large timber gate blocking the ranch entrance. The gate had a beautiful wood carving of a horse over the top.

"Now what?" Jo asked.

"The gate doesn't appear to be locked. Let me get out and try to open it."

Wyatt released the latch and pushed the heavy gate open enough for Jo to pull through. She drove the van through the opening, then stopped and waited for Wyatt to close the gate behind them and get back inside the van.

Jo took in the scenery around them. "Wow! This place is something. Toto, I don't think we're in Kansas any more," she said.

"You can say that again. I guess Carson's family is very well off," Wyatt said.

The dirt lane was accented by a rustic wooden fence. A large horse stable was located off to one side in the distance. On the other side, cows roamed in the vast pasture land. The rolling hills went on forever until they reached the base of majestic mountains covered in snow. A large log home greeted them at the end of the driveway.

"If I was going to hide out I would sure choose this place," Jo said.

"Let's hope you're right and Carson is here."

Jo slowly drove down the driveway, leaving a cloud of dust behind. She came to a stop in front of the house. "Your destiny awaits. Let's just hope you get the answers you're looking for."

"Why don't you stay in the van with Moose until I find out if Carson is even here?"

Moose sat at attention in the front seat, watching Wyatt's every move as he rang the doorbell. It seemed like forever before a nice looking lady answered the door. "That must be Carson's adoptive mother," Jo told Moose. Jo watched as a man joined them and shook Wyatt's hand. "That looks like a good sign." Then Wyatt turned and walked back to the van.

"Well, what did they say?" Jo asked eagerly as Wyatt moved Moose over so there was enough room for him to sit.

Wyatt was a bit preoccupied as Moose happily licked his face to show his affection. He wiped his face with his sleeve and gave Moose a big hug to show how much he loved him. "Carson's father told me he's staying at their cabin in the mountains." He held up a piece of paper. "And he gave me the address," he said with a smile.

"You sweet talker you."

Wyatt opened the Idaho map they had bought at the gas station and laid it across the dashboard. "It doesn't look that far away. We should be there by lunch. It feels great to finally be making some progress. I just hope Carson will talk to me once we find him. He may not be as welcoming as his mother."

"I take it you didn't tell her he may be your brother?"

"No, let me first figure out if he's trying to kill me, then I'll broach the subject that we might be related. Have you checked your phone for any messages from the sheriff?"

"No. I didn't want to give anyone a chance to track us. Let me turn it on real quick and see if there are any messages." Jo quickly powered up her phone. "I have one message!" She quickly tapped her phone and placed it on speaker so Wyatt could hear the message.

"The men I arrested last night turned out to be undercover ATF officers. They said they received a tip that indicated your address was involved with trafficking of weapons. They wouldn't tell me who provided them with the tip, but I told them they were clearly misled. I had to let them go. Watch your back." The call ended and Jo turned off her phone before it could be tracked.

"Someone is really going out of their way to set you up."

"Yeah, I'm not sure if that's it."

"What do you mean?"

"Someone obviously thinks I remember more than I do. They may be trying to send me a message to keep my mouth shut."

"So you think if we had been home when ATF raided my house, we might have accidentally been shot while trying to evade capture?"

"Yeah, something like that, or at least that would've been their story. I feel there's something big going on here and someone is trying to cover it up. Somehow I'm in the middle of all this and I just need to find out why. Let's just hope Carson can give me some answers."

★★★

The cabin was located deep in the woods, down a bumpy dirt road, isolated from all human contact. Jo approached the cabin cautiously and stopped the van to search for anything suspicious before pulling up to the front porch. "There doesn't seem to be any signs of life. I don't see a vehicle. Do you think he left?"

"He may not want anyone to know he's here. Why don't you keep the vehicle running just in case you need to get away fast? I'll knock on the front door and see if anyone answers."

"I'm not leaving without you."

"If things go terribly wrong, get out of here with Moose as fast as you can. You won't be able to help me if you're dead."

Wyatt stepped out of the vehicle and slowly walked up the steps to the front door. His 9 mm handgun was hidden under his jacket and provided him with some assurance of protection. If Carson wanted to kill him, this would be the perfect location. We should have told someone where we were going, Wyatt thought to himself. The curtains were drawn across the front windows so he couldn't see inside. He knocked on the door and stood off to the side in case Carson shot through the door. There was no response. Wyatt tried a different approach. "Carson, this is Wyatt

114

from Afghanistan! I mean you no harm! I just want to talk with you!" Wyatt yelled at the door.

Wyatt listened intently, then heard the deadbolt on the door being released. The door opened and Wyatt stared down the barrel of a shotgun. Wyatt placed his hands in the air.

"Are you alone?"

"A friend and my dog are in the van," Wyatt responded calmly.

"How did you find me?"

"Your father gave me your address."

"What do you want?"

"Someone has been trying to kill me. I thought you might be able to help me figure out who by telling me what happened the day I was injured in Afghanistan."

Carson lowered his rifle. "Pull the van in the garage so it won't be seen. I'll open the garage door for you."

Wyatt returned to the van. "Park in the garage," he told Jo.

"Then what, does he plan on killing us and disposing of our bodies in the woods?"

"I hope not."

"You didn't sound very convincing."

"He may be a little paranoid, but I don't think he'll harm us. Just follow my lead once we're inside."

They did as instructed and entered the house through the windowless garage. They stepped inside and found themselves in a large kitchen area with a beautifully rustic stained oak table. Windows flanked the table on one side providing a spectacular view of the mountain in the distance. "Carson, I would like for you to meet Jo and Moose."

"What happened to Moose?"

"A stray bullet hit him in the shoulder."

"That's too bad," Carson said.

Wyatt thought Carson's concern for Moose sounded real.

"I used to have a German Shepherd when I was a boy. Moose reminds me of him. He was just as gorgeous. Where did you find him?" Carson asked as he held out his hand for Moose to smell before patting him.

"He was a gift from a volunteer organization who helps soldiers deal with PTSD." The look in Carson's eyes told Wyatt he wasn't the only one dealing with the aftermath of Afghanistan.

"Sorry for the greeting, but I wasn't expecting you."

"We didn't mean to surprise you, but didn't have a way to contact you to give you a heads up that we were coming."

"Can I get you something to drink? I just made a fresh pot of coffee."

"Yes, that would be great. Do you have a bowl I can put some fresh water in for Moose?"

Carson filled two coffee mugs and set them on the counter. "There's a sugar bowl on the table and cream in the refrigerator if you would like some with your coffee. Here's a bowl you can use for Moose."

Jo spoke up. "I could use some cream." She helped herself and opened the refrigerator door. She searched for the creamer, amazed at how much food was inside. It looked like he had just raided a grocery store. There were several different types of juice, all kinds of fruit and vegetables, every kind of meat you could imagine from steaks to chicken, and two gallons of milk. How could one man eat so much food?

Carson stepped around Jo, located the creamer, and handed it to her before quickly closing the refrigerator.

Wyatt filled the bowl Carson gave him for Moose half full of water and set it on a rug in front of the sink so he wouldn't slobber water all over the nice hardwood floors.

"Have a seat." Carson motioned to a brown leather sofa in the family room.

Jo took in the beautiful decor. There were high wooden ceilings with exposed giant beams and a rustic stairwell leading to a loft area. An elk stared back at her, mounted on the far wall, and a large bear rug covered the floor in front of a massive stone fireplace. "This is quite a place," she told Carson.

"Thanks. My family has owned this since I was a kid. We used to come up here in the summers. We entertained ourselves by hiking, hunting, playing board games, and watching old DVD movies. There was never television, with the reception being so bad in the mountains."

"That doesn't sound like a bad way to spend your summers," Wyatt said.

"What brings you to my part of the world."

"Like I was saying, someone has been trying to kill me and I think it has something to do with Afghanistan. I was hoping you could tell me about the day I was injured. My memory of the events leading up to when I was wounded aren't very clear. I know there was an explosion and that Rob was killed, but I don't know how." He left out what Jeff Armer had told him about it being his gun that killed Rob. He wanted to see what Carson knew first.

Carson hesitated and looked at Jo.

"If you would feel more comfortable speaking to me alone, Jo can go in another room where she can't overhear the details of that day."

"That would probably be best. Why don't you help yourself to something to eat in the kitchen? There is bread in the pantry if you want to make yourself a sandwich."

Jo was disappointed, but didn't want to discourage Carson from telling Wyatt what had happened. She disappeared into the kitchen.

Carson spoke softly. "Your life isn't the only one in danger. They're also after me."

"Who is after you?" Wyatt asked quietly.

"I'm not sure, but it definitely has something to do with Afghanistan."

"Start from the beginning and tell me why you think this has something to do with our time in Afghanistan."

"Do you remember that mission where we delivered some weapons to a group of rebels that were fighting against the Taliban?"

"Yes. We approached the rebel's secret location in the cover of darkness and quickly offloaded the weapons as instructed, then got out of there before we could be discovered by the Taliban."

"Somehow those weapons ended up in a cargo plane headed for the United States"

"And how do you know this?"

"I'm getting ahead of myself. Let me go back to the night you were injured. Our assignment was to investigate a possible location where the Taliban fighters might be hiding. Our source said a strategic planning meeting was taking place the night of our mission. We arrived and it was eerily quiet and there wasn't a soul around. It was almost like someone told them we were coming. A school was located about half a klick away. I saw a flash of light in the window and decided to check it out. I went alone and snuck in the back of the building. I heard voices coming from down the hall. I slowly approached the room where the voices were coming from. I peered through a crack in the wall. There were two men and a woman talking inside. I tried to make out what they were saying."

"I remember!" Wyatt said. "Rob and I saw you heading toward the school and decided to check out the building. We followed you and heard the same voices coming from down the hall. You were nowhere in sight, though. We approached the room, but then my memory gets foggy again."

"I turned to leave out the back when I heard a commotion coming from behind me. The two men I saw in the room must have heard you approaching and were attacking you. I rushed to help but before I could get close enough, your attacker had you on the ground. Next, I heard your weapon fire. Rob fell to the ground. I managed to scare away the men, but I knew many more would be coming. I told you to pick up Rob and run. I needed to create a diversion. I rushed back down the hall and tossed a grenade in one of the rooms. I ran out the back of the building just as the explosion rocked me to my core. I was dazed, but not seriously injured. By the time I made my way around front, the rest of the team had quickly gathered and they had your body loaded on a makeshift stretcher. Rob was draped over the shoulder of another marine. The team managed to make it back to the hidden vehicles without anyone else being injured. We radioed for a helicopter and it met us about 10 kilometers from our location. You were whirled away. Rob never had a chance. He was killed instantly from a bullet wound to the head."

"You do realize your diversion just about killed me?"

"That was not my intent. There must've been some combustable or explosive material being stored in the room where I threw the grenade. It shouldn't have caused so much destruction."

118

"So I did kill Rob?"

"Obviously it wasn't on purpose, and who's to say your finger was even on the trigger when it fired."

"Why did you tell Shaun, Rob's brother, that I killed him?"

"At the time, I was just angry over the whole situation. The commander came down hard on me for destroying the school and putting innocent civilians in danger. I thought by setting off an explosion in the school, it would cause enough of a distraction to give us time to get safely away. After the incident, I was given leave while it was being investigated. I decided not to return."

"You're AWOL?"

"I guess you could call it that."

"You didn't think that would be a problem?"

"Like I said, there is something else going on here. Why would weapons we delivered to the rebels end up on a cargo plane headed for the US?"

"Yeah, you never did explain how the schoolhouse bombing and the weapons were related."

"A few days after the incident, the commander notified the unit our tour was being cut short and we were all being shipped home. I traveled back to the states on a military cargo plane. Being stuck in the back of the noisy cargo airplane for such a long journey was starting to wear on me, so I got up to stretch my legs while most of the guys slept. I walked to the rear of the aircraft where the cargo was being stored. I noticed a crate with inconspicuous red tick marks on the side. It seemed strange to me that this was the only crate with those markings, and I got curious. I managed to jimmy the lid off of the crate. You can imagine my surprise when I saw it was full of weapons. Remember the rifles we delivered to the rebels had a black engraved plate attached to the butt of the gun to identify its origin?"

"Yes, I remember."

"These weapons had the same plate like the ones we delivered to the rebels. So when we landed in Texas, I hid in the shadows and watched as the cargo was offloaded. The crate with the weapons was immediately transferred to the back of a dark colored panel truck. The truck pulled away as soon as the back doors were closed. I couldn't get what I saw out of my mind. So the next day, I stopped by the base commander's office and expressed my concerns about the weapons possibly being smuggled into this country. My concern was noted, but the base commander didn't seem to be alarmed. He said he would check the manifest for anything out of the ordinary. Then about a month ago I start getting these strange emails. They implied that they knew my secret and I better watch my back. I tried to track the source of the emails, with no luck. That's why I'm hiding out here. I don't want to put my parents in any danger."

"Maybe the emails are just referring to the fact that you're AWOL?"

"No, I don't think that's it. There is a skull and crossbones symbol at the end of the message. No one would want me dead just because I'm AWOL."

"Did you tell anyone else about seeing the weapons on the airplane?"

"No one other than the base commander, and he basically told me not to worry, that the shipment was probably being transported to another base for distribution. He didn't seem the least bit surprised that the weapons were on the airplane and that they were transferred to a suspicious vehicle."

Suddenly there was a chirping noise coming from Carson's laptop laying on the coffee table in front of him. Carson quickly opened the laptop.

"They found us! They must have followed you here."

"Who found us?"

Carson turned the laptop so Wyatt could see. There were security cameras located in the woods around the property. They were currently recording several men with guns approaching.

"We've got to get out of here!" Wyatt said.

"It's too late. They'll kill you if you try to escape. Get Jo and follow me."

Carson slid back the bear rug and revealed a hidden door in the floor. "My parents were survivalists and thought it would be a good idea to have a safe room just in case. Grab Jo and Moose and climb down the stairs."

Wyatt went to the kitchen and motioned for Jo to follow him. "Hurry, someone is coming! We don't have much time."

"What's going on?" Jo asked.

"We've been discovered. Follow me," Wyatt said.

"There is a light switch at the bottom of the stairs. I'll be down as soon as I secure everything up here," Carson said.

Wyatt carried Moose down the dimly lit stairwell, and Jo followed close behind. He switched on the light, and they were left standing speechless at what they saw.

A large, fully furnished room, including a kitchen, bathroom, and large built-in gun cabinet filled with weapons stood in front of them.

"Wow, this is amazing! It looks like they have their own armory," Jo said.

Wyatt looked at the wall of weapons stored off to the side of the room. Before he could say anything, Carson closed the door behind him and raced down the stairs.

"The bear rug will slide back in place, concealing the entrance to the safe room. My parents fully stocked this place so you could survive down here for years if there was a nuclear attack. It has its own isolated ventilation system for generating clean air so no contaminates can enter this room."

"Were your parents planning on World War III?" Jo asked.

"Like I said, they wanted to make sure they could protect themselves."

"This place is great, but we can't hole up down here forever. Someone is bound to figure out where we are hiding," Jo said.

"The door is bolted from inside and virtually invisible from outside. The floor planks line up perfectly so no opening is evident." Carson stepped over to a wall with a large screen and pushed the power button. Immediately the images from the many cameras placed around the perimeter of the property were displayed. Carson zoomed in on one of the men approaching the house. The letters ATF were displayed across his back.

"This might be a good time to mention that Jo's house was raided by two supposed ATF agents just two nights ago. The only difference was, they were wearing street clothes and claimed to be undercover ATF agents. I don't like this. It can't be a coincidence that they have shown up here," Wyatt shared.

"Don't worry, they won't find anything but an empty cabin and then will leave. Just be patient," Carson said.

They stared at the screen as the men tried to break through the heavy, solid wood front door.

"They're going to find our van and know we are somewhere close," Wyatt added, starting to feel trapped.

"Unlikely. While you were retrieving Jo from the kitchen, I pressed a switch that activated an elevator in the garage. Your van was lowered below ground, concealing it from view. If they look in the garage all they'll see is empty space."

"Man, your parents thought of everything," Jo said.

They watched as the ATF officers gave up breaking down the front door and tried to enter through a window.

"The windows are all made of bulletproof glass and are virtually impenetrable," Carson added.

"This is more a fortress than a vacation cabin," Wyatt said.

"You might as well relax. We may have to stay down here for a while to make sure the coast is clear before you attempt to leave."

Wyatt didn't like feeling trapped and started to pace. Moose sensed Wyatt's anxiety and rubbed up against him for attention, a maneuver Moose was trained to do to help Wyatt's mind focus on something other than his predicament. Wyatt stopped pacing and sat on the floor next to Moose. Moose laid across his lap and Wyatt proceeded to stroke his smooth coat, which helped him relax.

Jo watched this speechless interaction between the two and smiled at the bond they had for each other. She made herself comfortable in a recliner and listened to the banging from above as the men attempted to enter the cabin.

After about an hour, quiet finally filled the space as the men gave up their pursuit and left the property.

"Now what?" Jo asked.

"Now we wait till dark. I'll do a recon and make sure the coast is clear. There's an old logging road behind the cabin that few people know about. You should be able to leave without being seen, but it might be a little bumpy."

"What about you?" Wyatt asked.

"I have my own exit strategy. You don't need to worry about me. Is anyone hungry?" Carson asked.

"How can you think about food at a time like this?" Jo asked.

"A man has to eat to keep up his strength. Survival training 101 in military," Wyatt said. "You never know when your next meal may be so take advantage when food is available."

"There's plenty of hydrated concoctions to choose from and there is fresh water in the refrigerator. Help yourself."

Wyatt glanced through the selection. "Yum, roast beef and mashed potatoes," he said as he picked up the freeze dried packet. "Your turn," Wyatt said to Jo.

"Look, there's peach cobbler. That's my favorite," Jo said as she held up her selection.

"Leave it to you to have dessert first!" Wyatt joked.

They ate to pass the time. Jo broke the uneasy silence and leaned over and whispered in Wyatt's ear. "Don't you think you should tell him?"

Wyatt looked into Carson's eyes and decided he should share his news. "When we were trying to locate you, Jo did a little research online looking for information that might lead us to your whereabouts. She discovered that you were adopted by your parents. I was abandoned by my mother when I was young and raised in the foster care system. Jo dug a little deeper and was surprised to learn that both of our mother's have the same name, Lidi. With such an unusual name, I figured it couldn't just be a coincidence. It might be possible that we're brothers."

Carson was speechless while he tried to take in what he had just heard. "My parents never kept it a secret that I was adopted. As soon as I was old enough, they told me that my biological mother loved me so much she chose a better life for me and gave me up for adoption. It never occurred to me that I might have a brother."

Jo spoke up, "You both have blue eyes and blond hair, are about the same height and build, with a chiseled chin and dimples when you smile, which isn't often. The resemblance and similar mannerisms are uncanny. You're both right handed, uneasy in small spaces, and don't like to sit still for very long," she said as she watched them pacing back and forth from one end of the room to the other. "Anyone seeing you together would know you are related."

They walked over to the mirror above the sink in the bathroom. They looked intently at each other. "You could definitely be my brother. I don't know why I didn't see it before now," Carson said.

"Well, for starters we didn't spend a lot of time together in the unit. We both kept pretty much to ourselves and did our job," Wyatt said.

"That's what we have to do now. We can't let anyone know we are brothers. Tonight we go our separate ways. That's the only way you will stay safe," Carson said.

"There has to be another way. I don't want to spend the rest of my life looking over my shoulder, worried that I'll be discovered and killed," Wyatt said.

"I have a plan to expose whoever is doing this."

"Great! Then let me help. I can cover your back."

"You're still recovering from your injuries and you need to hole up someplace where you won't be found."

"Nonsense. My head is as good as it is going to get. Sitting around worrying about when I'll be discovered is not going to make me any stronger."

"What I'm proposing is not exactly legal and could get you in a whole heap of trouble."

"It can't be any worse than the trouble I'm already in."

"In that case, you need to get Jo and Moose someplace safe. They can't be tied to what we're about to do."

Wyatt looked over at Jo. "You know he's right. You have already stuck your neck out too much for me. You and Moose will return to Wheeler on your own. I'll ride with you long enough to get you back to the main road and then I'll disappear. I know you'll take good care of Moose if I don't return."

"There has to be another way. We need to discuss this. We can go to the FBI and convince them you're being set up and they can help catch whoever is behind this."

"I don't think I could trust the FBI with people associated with ATF trying to kill me. I think Carson is right. We have to expose this ourselves, and clear our names. That's the only way we'll ever be free."

Jo didn't like this one bit, but knew arguing with Wyatt at this moment wouldn't get him to change his mind. Night was quickly approaching.

"Why don't you lie down in the back and try to get some rest? You have a long drive home and I don't want you falling asleep behind the wheel," Wyatt said.

Jo laid down on top of a cot that was set up in the back room. She was exhausted, and tried to sleep. Her mind wouldn't shut down, though. She feared she would never see Wyatt again.

Chapter 13

"Okay, it's time. It has been dark now for several hours and there has been no movement outside. I'm going to check upstairs to make sure it is clear."

Carson left and Jo had a bad feeling in the pit of her stomach. She whispered to Wyatt, "Carson may be your brother, but I'm not convinced he won't kill you as soon as I'm gone. Are you sure you want to go through with this?"

Before Wyatt could answer, Carson opened the trap door and told them, "The coast is clear."

Carson didn't want to turn on lights which might alert someone of their presence. Wyatt climbed the dimly lit stairwell first with Moose in his arms. He set Moose down softly at the top of the landing then extended his hand to Jo to steady her up so she wouldn't trip.

"I've raised your van back to ground level. I'll open the back garage door so you can drive toward the logging road without being seen. Go straight for about one hundred yards then you'll see a path through the trees. There is just enough moonlight for you to drive slowly down the mountain without turning on your headlights. Once you're back to the main road, have Jo drop you off at the tavern located at the bottom of the mountain. There are no cameras installed there that might record your location." Carson looked at his watch. "I'll plan to meet you at the tavern by 2AM. That'll give you plenty of time to get down the mountain and for me to gather a few things we'll need. If I don't show, that means something went wrong and you're on your own."

Wyatt nodded, indicating he understood. Without another word spoken Jo, Wyatt, and Moose climbed back into the van. Wyatt decided he better drive in case they ran into trouble. He started the engine and slowly left the safety of the garage. He did as instructed and drove straight for about one hundred yards and then he saw the clearing that Carson indicated would lead them to the logging road. He slowly drove down the rough road, bumping

126

along at about twenty miles per hour. The road wound back and forth losing elevation with each turn. He carefully made each turn to keep from skidding off the mountain.

Jo stayed quiet and held onto the armrest for dear life. After what seemed like an eternity, Wyatt turned onto the blacktop. Jo breathed a huge sigh of relief. "Well, that was exciting."

"We aren't free and clear yet. Let's just hope the men after us haven't put up a roadblock, hoping to catch us."

After about ten miles Jo spoke up, "There's the tavern!"

Wyatt pulled into the parking lot. It was full of cars and they could hear music blaring from inside. He left the engine running and put the van in park. "Well, I guess this is it."

"I'm not going anywhere until I'm sure Carson is coming for you, so you might as well turn off the engine and sit tight," Jo said.

"That's nonsense. You need to get as far away as you can while you are still alert enough to drive. If Carson doesn't show, I'll find my way back to Wheeler."

Jo didn't move. "I have a bad feeling about this. Call it women's intuition if you want, but I don't trust Carson. Who keeps that much food in the refrigerator for one person? I don't think he's telling you everything."

"You don't trust Carson because his refrigerator has food?"

"Not just because of that, I don't know what he told you about what happened in Afghanistan while I was in the kitchen mesmerized by all the food, but that doesn't make him any less of a suspect. You saw the arsenal of weapons he has in his safe room. He could very well be trafficking weapons and that's why the officials are looking for him. What's to say he won't kill you after he picks you up? You're his only witness."

"I guess you have a point. I might be putting too much faith in him just because we served together."

"After Carson shared with you what happened the night you were injured, did any of your memory come back?"

"I remembered seeing Carson running toward the schoolhouse where I was injured and where Rob was killed. We were following Carson. That was the reason we went to the schoolhouse. His version of events that night seems to make sense. Carson said that Rob and I were attacked and he saved me, but I just don't remember what happened after I entered the schoolhouse."

"Is it possible that Carson is testing to see exactly what you do remember? Could his version of the events that night be slightly off so he could determine what your reaction would be?"

"I guess it's possible, but I have no reason to doubt what he told me wasn't true."

"I'm going to give you another scenario of what could have possibly happened and see what you think. Let's just say that Carson is behind what has happened to you. You saw him at the schoolhouse doing something he shouldn't have been. He tries to cover it up by killing you and Rob. But miraculously you survive. Now he's worried that you might tell someone the truth. He goes to Rob's memorial service and tells Shaun, Rob's brother, you killed Rob, knowing Shaun will come after you to revenge his brother's death. When that doesn't work, he lures you to Old Mill Pond Road so he can finish you off himself. When that fails, he makes an anonymous call to the bureau to tell them you are trafficking weapons. He figures if he can't kill you, he can at least have you arrested and put behind bars, where even if you did remember what happened, no one would believe you due to your head injury. How is my version sounding so far?"

Wyatt hated to admit to himself that Jo may be onto something. "All right, let's say that Carson is behind what is happening to me. Why wouldn't he just kill us while we were at his cabin and bury our bodies in the woods?"

"Obviously his parents knew that we came to see him. If we suddenly went missing and our faces were plastered all over the news, don't you think his parents would become suspicious? He has to find a way for you to disappear so no one will suspect him, and if that means coming up with a ruse so you believe you are helping him find the real perpetrator, so be it."

"If you're correct, then that's why the men wearing ATF jackets showed up at his cabin. Maybe they figured out he was the one really trafficking weapons and who gave them the anonymous tip leading them to me."

"Now you're thinking!"

"So you think his real plan is to pick me up at 2AM and get rid of me for good, so I can't reveal what happened in Afghanistan."

"Yup, that pretty much sums it up."

Wyatt looked at his watch and put the van in drive. "It's 1:30AM. We need to get out of here before Carson shows up. I'll drive the first leg so you can rest."

"That still leaves us with a problem. Where do we go where Carson won't find you?"

"I think our original plan of using me as bait to catch whoever is after me was a good one. If he decides to hunt me down, we'll be ready for him. I'll put some security measures in place so we can catch him before he, or whoever, can kill me first. Now try to rest. I'll wake you up in a few hours and we can switch."

They stayed on the back roads the whole time, just in case Carson or the authorities were looking for them. They didn't dare let their guard down.

***

Tired and weary, Jo and Wyatt arrived at Burt's garage in Wheeler just before 3PM. "Thanks for letting us use the van," Jo told Burt, handing him the keys.

"No problem."

Wyatt glanced around the parking lot at the numerous cars waiting to be serviced. "Looks like business is good."

"You can say that. I think half of the town decided they needed their car serviced this week."

"I'm a pretty good mechanic, if you could use some help," Wyatt offered.

"What kind of experience do you have?"

"I've always enjoyed tinkering with cars to discover how they work. In high school I took shop class and rebuilt an entire engine. I also did some vehicle maintenance in the military before joining Special Forces."

"I could start you off with changing oil and rotating tires until I can see for myself what you're capable of. If that wouldn't be an issue, when can you start?"

"How about in the morning?"

"Sounds good. I can't promise you there'll be enough work to keep you employed full time, but I could use your help to catch up."

"That isn't an issue. I can arrange my schedule to meet your needs." Wyatt shook Burt's greasy hand to seal the deal.

Once back inside Jo's truck, she asked, "What are you doing?"

"I'm trying to make a little money so I can buy a car and get back on my feet."

"I mean, isn't it dangerous working where Carson can find you?"

"Like I said, I can't spend the rest of my life hiding. If Carson wants to find me he will, regardless if I'm working or not. I just have to stay alert and be ready when he does. That being said, does Wheeler have an electronics store where we can pick up some security cameras and a home alarm system?"

"Yes, Stan's hardware sells just about anything you may need. The selection may be limited compared to the large box stores, but he can order whatever you need if he doesn't have it."

"Then let's stop at Stan's before we return to your place."

"I also need to run by my Dad's store to let him know we're back. I guess I'll be returning to work tomorrow."

"Just keep an eye out for any new customers that don't look like they belong in Wheeler. Make sure you keep your gun with you at all times. Also, keep Moose with you. At the sight of him most people change their mind about trying anything."

Jo rolled her eyes and looked over at Wyatt. "Being a little over protective aren't we?"

"I'm just saying I've gotten used to having you around and would hate for something to happen to you."

Jo smiled, realizing Wyatt cared for her more than he wanted to admit. "I would feel better, though, if Moose stayed with you. No one has a reason to kill me and Moose would alert you if someone wanted to cause you harm."

"We'll see," Wyatt said as Jo pulled up to her Dad's store.

"I'll just be a minute," Jo said as she jumped out of the truck and went inside.

"Well, look who decided to let us know she's still alive," Jo's Dad said sarcastically when she entered the store.

"I'm sorry. Wyatt and I were so busy the last two days I didn't have a chance to call."

"Did he find his friend in the military and get the answers he was looking for?"

"Yes, he discovered some information he didn't know before."

"Hopefully there won't be any more ATF agents knocking down your door."

"I'll have to stop by and thank Charlie for clearing up that mess for me. I've got to run, but wanted to let you know I plan to return to work tomorrow," Jo said as she walked out the door.

Jo jumped back inside her truck and was greeted with a lick from Moose. She gave him a hug and a kiss on top of the head. "It's so nice to know you still love me even though Wyatt is back. I don't know about you but I'm starved. How about we run by the hardware store and then pick up a pizza on the way home?"

"I could use some food and I'm sure Moose could devour a bowl or two."

Moose barked to acknowledge he was hungry as well.

Jo pushed the shopping cart while Wyatt pitched in four motion sensor lights and cameras, along with an alarm system.

"No one should be able to enter the house undetected once these are installed."

After checking out, Jo picked up a large meat lover's pizza. The tantalizing pizza smell had Moose drooling all over the truck seat before they even left the parking lot. He just about flooded the truck cab by the time they arrived home.

After supper, Wyatt used what little energy he had left to install the motion sensor lights and cameras. He quickly rigged an alarm system so if anyone tried to open the doors or windows they would be alerted.

He collapsed on the sofa next to Jo. "I'm bushed. I think I could sleep for a week."

"You and me both. I'm going to run through the shower and fall into bed."

"I know this will sound like I'm being a macho man, but I would feel more comfortable if we slept in the same room. I promise I won't try anything and, if you like, I can sleep on the floor with Moose."

"Don't be ridiculous. I kinda like that you want to protect me. I would also sleep easier with you and Moose close by. My bed is big enough for you and Moose. Go get cleaned up in the guest room and move your stuff in here with me."

Jo washed two days of grime out of her hair and brushed her teeth. She opened the bathroom door to find Wyatt sound asleep in her bed with Moose stretched across her side of the bed. She shoved Moose over a little, which gave her just enough space to lie on her side without falling out of the bed. She had to admit, it was nice having someone near who cared about her and wanted to protect her.

***

Jo rolled off the bed onto the floor as the siren sounding alarm on Wyatt's cell phone broke the silence. "What the crap is that? You just about gave me a heart attack."

"I'm sorry. I didn't want to be late for my first day of work." Wyatt offered Jo his hand and lifted her off the floor. Standing close together he looked into her eyes and smiled.

Jo didn't like his mischievous look. "What are you smiling about?"

"I've never seen your hair in such a state," Wyatt laughed.

Jo glanced at her image in the mirror over her dresser. Her hair was sticking straight up in the back. "I was too tired to dry it last night and went to bed with it still soaking wet," she said as she tried to push it down with her hand.

Wyatt kissed her on the cheek. "I still love you," came out of his mouth before he realized what he was saying. Before Jo could respond, he disappeared to go get dressed.

Jo stood there speechless, not sure if she had heard him right. "Did he say he loves me?" Jo mumbled to herself. "How do I feel? Obviously, I have feelings for him," she said, answering her own question. "Since I didn't say anything in response, is he going to think I don't care about him? I just wasn't expecting him to say it so soon." Moose broke the conversation with herself with a bark. "I'm sorry, you need to go out, don't you boy?" She opened the back door and Moose sprang out the door, full of energy, not letting the splint hinder him from clearing the back yard of squirrels.

Watching Moose running and having fun reminded her just how much her life had changed in such a short time. She suddenly realized how much she loved Moose and Wyatt and how heartbroken she would be if they ever left.

"You're not dressed yet?" Wyatt stated the obvious. "You have to drop me off at work."

"I'm sorry, my mind is still in a fog this morning. Why don't you start some coffee and feed Moose while I change?" Jo said as she rushed from the kitchen.

"I think I can handle that," Wyatt said.

Jo reappeared dressed in jeans, a work shirt, and tennis shoes. She tamed her hair by pulling it back in a ponytail and dabbed a little makeup on her face to cover the dark circles under her eyes.

"Ready to go?" Wyatt asked as he handed her a mug of coffee.

"I am now," Jo said as she swallowed a big gulp of heavenly caffeine. "Oh, I didn't even make you breakfast. Do you want to stop by the drive thru and pick up a sausage biscuit on the way to work?"

"Sounds like the breakfast of champions," Wyatt joked.

"I promise, I'll stop by the grocery store on the way home and stock up on some healthy fruit and vegetables for you. I know you're still healing from your injury and should be eating healthier than what we have been lately."

"This body can run on just about anything. Believe me, what we've been eating is just fine."

Jo pulled into Burt's garage just as Burt was opening the shop doors. "See, no problem. I got you here right on time."

Wyatt rolled his eyes at Jo, realizing she probably has never been on time for anything in her life. "You keep Moose like we discussed. I can't have him underfoot or he'll be covered in grease by the end of the day, and he could get hurt."

Jo didn't like leaving Wyatt unprotected, but knew he was probably right about Moose's safety.

Wyatt leaned over and rubbed the top of Moose's head. "You watch after Jo today and don't let anything bad happen to her."

Moose barked in response, as if he understood. Wyatt closed the truck door and Jo watched as he walked to the car bay.

She pulled away with an empty feeling in the pit of her stomach. This was the first time they had been apart since he came home from the hospital. It felt like a piece of her was missing. How did she let herself become so attached to someone in such a short time?

Jo was greeted by her Dad as she entered the store, "So, if it isn't the prodigal daughter returned to take her place by her father's side," he joked.

"Oh, Dad. I haven't been gone that long."

"I missed you sweetheart, and just glad to have you and Moose back. I'm surprised to see him with you."

"Wyatt started a new job working for Burt's garage today and thought Moose would be safer here with me." She left it at that and didn't bring up the possible threat that may still exist against her and Wyatt's lives.

"I'm glad to hear Wyatt's feeling well enough to work."

"Wyatt is a lot like you when you're sick. He can't stand to lie around and take it easy."

Jo looked up as the bell above the door rang. It was Sheriff Charlie. "How can I help you today, sheriff?" Jo asked.

"My wife needs some new spark plugs for her van."

"Let me get those for you," Jo offered. She stepped in the back of the store and returned a short time later. "Here we go," Jo said as she started to ring up the order.

"Did you see any more suspicious characters around your house last night?" Charlie asked.

"No, it was quiet, thank goodness. We were both so exhausted I don't know if we would have heard anyone even if they had broken in. Why don't I take these to your car for you?" Jo offered. She wanted to go outside to talk where her Dad could not overhear her conversation.

"It's nice to have such special service, but I get the feeling taking my spark plugs to my car is not the real reason you walked with me."

"Wyatt would be upset if he knew I told you, but I have some information I think you need to know. Wyatt has a military friend whose name is Carson Marshall. His family owns a big ranch in Idaho. Carson answered Wyatt's questions for him, but I'm not convinced what he told him was the truth. I think he may come after us, and I just wanted you to know in case something happens to either of us."

"Jo, I know you care for this young man, but have you considered he may need more help than you can provide?"

"What do you mean?"

"Until Wyatt remembers what really happened to him, you don't know if he could have been involved in something illegal. Whatever it is that he's mixed up in isn't going to resolve itself on its own. I get the impression he'll remain in danger until the other parties involved are caught. I'm worried for your safety."

"I know. That's why Wyatt installed motion sensors and cameras all around my house last night."

"That's all good, but cameras won't stop a bullet."

"I agree, but what more can we do?"

"I still have a good friend in the FBI, from my days on the New York City police force, that I would trust with my life. She is very good at helping witnesses remember details from a crime scene. How about I contact her and set up a meeting with Wyatt? Maybe she can help him remember what his brain has buried deep."

"It can't hurt. You set up the meeting and I'll make sure Wyatt arrives on time."

"I'll give her a call and let you know what I'm able to arrange," Charlie said as he climbed inside his cruiser and started to drive away.

Jo looked down at her hand and realized she was still holding the bag with the spark plugs inside. "Wait! I still have your spark plugs!" she yelled.

Charlie rolled down his window and took the package. "Thanks. I'm starting to get forgetful in my old age," Charlie joked.

Jo walked back inside the store and realized her Dad was staring at her. "What was that about?"

"I was just talking to Charlie about our trip," Jo lied.

"Somehow I find that hard to believe. I know when you are trying to hide something from me."

"I just don't want you to worry."

"It's my job to worry as a parent. I know I can't always be there to protect you but that doesn't mean I don't want to be. I do know I can't help you if you don't tell me what is going on."

"I didn't lie to you. Wyatt did meet his military friend, Carson Marshall, and was told what happened when he was injured in Afghanistan. But while we were visiting with him, men wearing ATF jackets raided his cabin deep in the woods. We hid in a safe room so no one saw us there. Carson said he had received death threats and was being set up just like Wyatt. I'm not sure I believe him, though. Since Wyatt admitted to Carson that he doesn't remember what happened the day he was injured, Carson could have told him anything and Wyatt would have no reason to doubt it was true. The sheriff was just telling me he knows someone that works for the FBI that might be able to help Wyatt regain his memory from that day. Maybe if he can find out what really happened to him the night he was injured and lost his best friend, then we can resolve this once and for all. Charlie is going to try to set up a meeting for us."

"It sounds like you could still be in danger."

"It's possible that someone is still out there that doesn't want Wyatt to remember what happened. That's why it is so important for Wyatt to meet with the FBI. If he can recall what led up to his injury and how Rob was killed, then maybe the police can catch whoever is behind the death threats."

Before Jo's Dad could protest, another customer entered the store. Jo didn't recognize the man. She suddenly felt uneasy at remembering what Wyatt had said about staying alert if an unfamiliar face appeared in the store. "Can I help you?" Jo asked, trying to remain calm.

"I'm lost and was hoping you could give me some directions," the man said.

At the sound of the man's voice, Moose lifted himself up off the ground beside Jo, using his one good hind leg, placed his front paws on top of the counter, and started to growl.

The man stepped back as Jo's Dad spoke up. "I'm sorry, he has never done that before."

"He must sense that I'm not much of a dog person," the man said as he backed out of the store.

"That's strange. He didn't stay long enough for us to provide him with the directions he needed," Jo's Dad said.

Jo watched as the man pulled out of the parking lot driving a beige Camry. She jotted down his license plate number.

"You think he may be someone trying to find Wyatt?"

"Think about it, Dad. Moose has never been aggressive toward anyone. I think Moose recognized the man's voice as someone that has threatened Wyatt in the past. I have to call Wyatt and warn him, then call Charlie and give the car description and license plate information."

"You call Burt's garage and I'll call Charlie," her Dad said taking the piece of paper from Jo's hand with the license plate information on it.

Wyatt tried to calm Jo down. "Whoever this guy was, he doesn't know where I am or he wouldn't have stopped by your store. Maybe he was just a guy asking for directions."

"I guess you're right, but if you could have seen Moose, he was ready to jump over the counter and attack this guy."

"Your store has a surveillance system, right?"

"Yes."

"Good. Show me the video tonight. Maybe I'll recognize the face."

"Hopefully Charlie will have a name by then."

"Listen, I have to get back to work. Don't worry. I'm sure he won't try to harm you now that he has seen Moose."

Wyatt hung up before Jo could say another word. She looked over at her Dad and he was still on the phone with Charlie. She kneeled down and praised Moose with hugs and kisses while she eagerly waited for her Dad to hang up the phone.

Finally the call ended and Jo's Dad spoke up. "He said the license plate is registered to a rent-a-car company. Charlie is going to call the company and find out who rented the vehicle."

Jo was disappointed that he wasn't able to find out more.

Her Dad could see her disappointment. "Let's just hope the guy is a lost tourist and doesn't mean you or Wyatt any harm. I don't want you leaving the store just in case his motives were not what they seemed. I'll make the deliveries today. You stay behind the counter with Moose. My gun is under the register, loaded and ready to shoot if you need it," he reminded Jo.

***

The day dragged by and Jo was still a bit uneasy. The phone rang as she was helping her Dad close out the register and she rushed to grab it.

"Hi Charlie! Did you discover the name of the person who rented the car?" Jo asked eagerly.

"No. The name given was fake, along with the driver's license. I got in contact with my friend at the FBI and told her it was urgent that Wyatt meet with her. She is driving down tonight and plans to meet Wyatt at my place at around 8PM."

"Great! Wyatt is working at Burt's garage. I'll pick him up after he gets off work and head over to your place."

"I'm not sure that's such a great idea. This guy in the rent-a-car may be waiting for you to leave work in hopes that you will lead him to Wyatt. I want you to have your Dad follow you to the police station. I'll pick up Wyatt from Burt's garage and meet you back in my office. You can leave your truck in the police parking lot where it'll be secure. Then we can all go to my house together in my car. You should be safe there. Wyatt can talk with my FBI friend and hopefully remember what happened. We'll decide what would be safest for you after that."

Jo did as instructed and drove to the police station after work, with her Dad following closely behind. She saw no signs of the beige Camry en route. She hoped Charlie's plan was going to work. Her Dad came inside the station with her and Moose. Moose drew attention from everyone in the office and ate up all the treats he was given while they waited for Wyatt and Charlie to arrive.

They finally came into view, walking down the hallway. Moose perked up and rushed over to greet Wyatt.

138

"I sure missed you today," Wyatt said as he rubbed Moose behind the ears. "I hear you did a good job of protecting Jo. You're such a good boy."

"Well, if you're ready, follow me to the back parking lot. We're going to sneak out using my wife's van just in case someone is watching for you."

"Call me when you know what your next move is," Jo's Dad spoke up.

"Will do." Jo leaned over and hugged his neck. "Try not to worry. Charlie will take good care of us."

Charlie pulled his wife's van up to the curb to limit the amount of time Wyatt and Jo would be in view of anyone watching. They, along with Moose, got inside, sinking down low in the back seat so no one would see them leave. Once they were far enough away from the station, they sat up and searched for any car that might be following them.

Charlie pulled into his garage and immediately closed the garage door behind him. Then he opened the side door to the van to let them out. "Come inside. I told my wife, Carol, that I was bringing company home so I'm sure she has a big supper waiting for us."

The aroma of garlic and tomato sauce accosted them when they stepped inside.

"I hope you're hungry. I made a large Italian casserole with plenty of fresh garlic bread and salad," Carol announced.

"I hope we're not inconveniencing you," Jo said.

"Not at all. I enjoy cooking."

"Wyatt, I would like for you to meet my wife Carol who has never had anyone leave her kitchen hungry," Charlie joked. He bent over and kissed his wife on the forehead.

"You can wash up in the hall bathroom," Carol said as she showed them the way. She looked down at Moose sitting at her feet in the hall. "And you must be Moose. My husband has been telling me how beautiful you are. Don't worry, I didn't forget about you. I fixed you something special for supper, also."

"We didn't mean for you to go to all this trouble," Wyatt said.

"Nonsense. It's no trouble. The house is too quiet since our kids grew up and moved away. You are welcome to stay as long as you need. There are extra towels in the linen closet right outside the bathroom if you need them."

"Charlie wouldn't happen to have an extra pair of pants I could wear, would he? I managed to get these a little greasy and don't want to mess up your furniture," Wyatt asked.

"I'm sure he can find something that'll fit you."

Jo helped Wyatt scrub the grease from under his nails. This was the first time they had been alone since that morning. "I hope you're not mad at me for getting Charlie and the FBI involved?"

"I want this to come to an end as much as you. I just hope I don't disappoint everyone if I'm still not able to remember what happened."

"Don't put any pressure on yourself. Whatever the outcome, I'm here until we get this resolved," Jo said as she kissed him on the cheek.

"Here you go. Try these on." Charlie handed Wyatt a pair of his sweats with a drawstring cord along the waist. Charlie was not a small man and probably figured the drawstring would be the only way to keep the pants from falling down to Wyatt's ankles.

Wyatt reappeared in the kitchen grease free wearing the baggy sweats. "We're going to have to put some meat on those bones," Carol said as she looked at his loose fitting sweats. "I hope you don't mind, but I picked up some canned dog food for Moose when Charlie said he would be coming with you."

"That's awful considerate of you. Moose will eat just about anything, but canned food is his favorite, and will be a nice treat for him."

"Here, I'll let you feed him while I put the food on the table. I placed a metal dog bowl we used for our German Shepherd in the laundry room. You can feed him in there."

"I was a canine officer for many years and my Shepherd saved my life more than once. Best dog I ever owned," Charlie said as his voice started to crack while remembering his special partner.

Jo and Wyatt ate until they thought their stomachs would explode. Then Carol announced, "Does anyone have room for cheesecake?"

Wyatt said, "I'll have to pass. You should have told me there was dessert before I had my second helping of casserole."

"No problem. Why don't we let supper settle and have dessert a little later with some coffee?"

"That sounds perfect, dear," Charlie said.

"Go into the family room to relax while I clean up the leftovers and put away the dishes," Carol said.

Jo stayed behind and helped clear the table and fill the dishwasher while Wyatt, Moose, and Charlie made themselves comfortable in the family room. By the time Jo and Carol joined them, they were out cold, sound asleep in the recliners. They woke when the doorbell rang announcing the arrival of Charlie's FBI friend.

Charlie quickly woke and opened the door. "Kate, it's so good to see you. Hopefully traffic wasn't too bad. I would like for you to meet Wyatt, Jo, and Moose."

"Nice to meet you all," Kate said as she extended her hand in a businesslike manner.

"Thanks for taking the time to come down here and meet with me," Wyatt said as he shook her hand.

"I know you've had a long drive, can I get you anything?" Carol asked.

"No, I'm fine. I'm afraid I need to drive back tonight, so is there someplace Wyatt and I can talk without any distractions?"

"Yes, of course. Use my office back here," Charlie said as he showed her the way.

***

Kate turned on the desk lamp and turned off the overhead light, giving the room a yellowish glow. She moved the swivel chair from around the desk and set it in front of where she planned to sit. "Have a seat," she instructed Wyatt. She didn't want any barriers between them. "Good. Now I want you to just relax, close your eyes, take a couple of deep breaths, and slowly exhale."

Wyatt did as instructed. "That's good. Charlie said you're having trouble remembering the details of your last mission. Whatever you tell me will not leave this room unless you want it to. Understand?"

Wyatt nodded his head up and down in acknowledgement.

"Why don't we start by you telling me what you can remember about that day?"

"It was a normal morning. I went to breakfast and then cleaned my weapon and checked my gear."

"Describe how you felt that morning."

"It was hot and dry as always. I hadn't sleep well that night. The sounds of bombs exploding in the distance kept me on edge."

"Who did you sit with at breakfast?"

"Rob. We normally ate breakfast together."

"Do you remember what you discussed?"

"Rob was having problems with his girlfriend back home. He hadn't heard from her in a week and he was worried she may have started dating someone else."

"How about you, did you have a girlfriend waiting for you at home?"

"No, the military was my family."

"After breakfast what did you do?"

"We were briefed on our next mission that was planned for that night."

"Was there anything unique about this mission?"

"No, not really. Members of the Taliban were believed to be hiding out in a nearby town. We were to search the building where they were supposedly staying."

"Do you remember anything out of the ordinary in preparing for this mission?"

"We waited until dark to leave. Most of the time we did our searches during the day, but depending on the circumstances, darkness provided us better cover."

"How many people participated in the mission?"

"There were eight of us."

"Did you always go with the same team?"

"Yes, our unit performed the missions together. Sometimes a man may be injured, or down with an illness that would prevent him from going, but all eight of us went on this mission."

"You said you left at nightfall. Did you encounter any resistance as you made your way to the town to check out the building where the Taliban were thought to be hiding?"

"I remember leaving our camp in a Humvee, but my memory gets sketchy after that."

"I would like to try to hypnotize you to help you remember. Would that be all right?"

"What do I have to do?"

"I want you to just relax. Close your eyes and take in a couple of deep breaths through your nose and slowly exhale through your mouth."

Wyatt did as instructed.

"Good. Now open your eyes and focus on the object in my hand. Concentrate on nothing but my voice as you feel yourself getting very sleepy. Your eyelids are growing so heavy. Don't fight the feeling. Close your eyes and continue to listen to my voice. I want you to go back to the night of your last mission. You are in your Humvee heading toward a town where the Taliban may be hiding. Can you tell me what you see?"

"It's dark. We stop our Humvees beside a ridge so we won't be seen. The team quietly hikes the rest of the way to town. There are many stars in the night sky to guide us. Our target comes into view. There are no visible lights inside the building. I put on my night vision goggles and search the area. I don't see a soul. Something doesn't feel right, though. It is too quiet. I fear we might be ambushed. Rob and I enter the building together. We turn to the right and clear each room on our side of the building. There is a scattering of furniture and rugs that indicates someone may have been there earlier in the day. Rob and I exit out the back and notice a light in the schoolhouse next door." Wyatt starts to breath heavily.

"You're safe," Kate reminded him. "You are watching yourself from a distance and can't get hurt. Continue with what happened when you reached the schoolhouse."

"We enter the schoolhouse and can hear voices in the distance speaking in English at the end of the corridor. We hide in the shadows and try to get close enough to hear what is being said. We find a hole in the wall and peer inside the room as the voices become louder." Wyatt hesitates.

"Remember, you can't be hurt. What do you see inside the room?"

143

"A woman dressed in a khimar. There are dead bodies of women and children on the floor all around her feet."

"Is there anyone else in the room with her?"

"Carson is there."

"Can you hear what they are saying?"

"Yes. The woman says, I made sure they knew you were coming so we could get the merchandise out without any resistance."

"I thought no one was supposed to get hurt."

"The Taliban raided the village down the road last night. I thought the bodies would help provide cover for what we did. They may be waiting to ambush you. You must go. The merchandise was placed in a World Aid vehicle and it's currently on the way to meet up with a cargo plane headed for the United States. I have someone in place to receive the cargo for us once the plane lands. Get out of here before we are discovered."

Wyatt suddenly covers his head with his arms and starts yelling, "No! Stop!"

"It's all right. Remember, you are watching yourself and can't be hurt. Continue, what is happening to you?"

"I'm hit over the head with an object and fall to my knees in agony. I'm dazed, but I get up and fight back. The attacker is struggling to get my rifle from my grasp. I knee him in the stomach and fall onto the ground on top of my assailant. He still has a tight grip on my weapon. My ears ache from the deafening sound as my rifle is discharged close to my head. I glance over at Rob and he is down. The man attacking me suddenly gives up the fight. He gets up and runs away. I look up and Carson is standing in front of me. He motions for me to grab Rob and get out of there. I lift Rob onto my shoulders. I turned back to look for Carson. He was running back down the corridor to the room where I had seen the dead bodies. He tossed a grenade inside. With all my remaining strength, I sprint for the exit door. Just as I reach the door I feel my body being hurled through the air. Rob and I hit the ground hard and debris rains over me. I can't breathe." Wyatt starts gasping for air.

Kate acted quickly, "Wyatt, listen to my voice. When I count to three I want you to wake up. You will remember what you saw but have no pain. One, two, three."

Wyatt jerks awake, not sure where he is. He is still trying to fill his lungs with air and is breathing rapidly.

"Wyatt, you're in Charlie's office. I want you to look into my eyes. Just take a deep breath." Kate breathed in slowly to show Wyatt what she wanted him to do.

Wyatt did as instructed.

"That's good. Breathe in and hold it. Now breathe out slowly. How do you feel?"

"Better, thanks."

"Do you still remember what you told me?"

Wyatt suddenly realized that he remembered. "Yes!"

"It sounded like you witnessed Carson talking to a woman who moved some merchandise from the area earlier that evening. The merchandise was transferred to a cargo plane on it's way to the United States."

"Carson lied. He told me I shot Rob and that isn't what happened. The man who attacked me is the one who pulled the trigger. Why would he do that?"

"He may not have been close enough to see what happened, or he was just testing you to find out exactly what you did remember. He probably didn't count on you surviving the explosion."

"Who do you think the woman was that he was talking with?"

"She may be someone that works for the World Aid group who was able to persuade Carson to help her smuggle something out of the country. While she was helping the people in the town, she must have discovered that the Taliban hid some valuable merchandise in the schoolhouse. She couldn't risk stealing it, though, with them close by. So she managed to get a message to your unit that the Taliban were hiding out in town. Then, from what you overheard, she made sure the Taliban knew you were coming so they would leave the area. She obviously needed some help with this plan and must have recruited Carson to make sure it went off without a hitch. But they didn't count on you and Rob overhearing what they had done. To help conceal his involvement,

Carson blew up the school. He thought he had eliminated his only witness, you."

Wyatt continued with the story. "I wake up from my coma, though, and to his dismay I recover. I disappear after rehab, not staying in one place very long. I don't get a driver's license or register a vehicle in my name so he isn't able to locate me. I do eventually get a cell phone, though, and Carson must have discovered my number and figured out where I was staying. I receive a text message telling me if I want the answers I've been searching for, meet in Wheeler off Old Mill Pond Road. I'm a bit suspicious, but go anyway. Once I get to Old Mill Pond Road I see a vehicle parked off to the side. I'm not sure what I'm about to find, so to be safe, I give Moose the stay command so he wouldn't try to leave the truck. As soon as I approach the vehicle a man jumps out and points a gun at my head and tells me to walk into the woods." Wyatt stops talking.

"What is it?"

"It isn't Carson. I don't recognize the man that got out of the vehicle."

"Maybe Carson has other accomplices. You overheard the woman say she had arranged for someone to meet the merchandise at the airport when it arrived in the US."

"I guess you are right. It just doesn't feel right."

"Continue. What happens after you walk into the woods with the man holding you at gunpoint?"

"I wasn't going to go down without a fight. The pond comes into sight and I figure that's how he's going to conceal my body. So before I reach the edge of the pond, I turn and attack my assailant. I manage to grab the wrist holding the gun. The gun falls to the ground as we continue to battle. I'm kicked in the stomach and bend over in misery which gives my assailant just enough time to reach the gun laying in the high grass. He pulls the trigger. I blacked out until I heard a soft voice calling my name. I wake up in the hospital." Wyatt is relieved, he is finally able to put the pieces together in his brain.

"What we don't know is what they smuggled into the United States and where it is now," Kate said.

146

"But we do know that Carson is involved," Wyatt added. "You know, I might have a clue as to what was smuggled."

"Good, we could use whatever info you have at this point."

"I met Carson at his parents' cabin in Idaho just two days ago. He told me when he returned to the states he witnessed a crate full of weapons being offloaded into the back of a delivery truck at the military base. He said he told the commanding officer, but didn't get an overwhelming response that he was going to investigate. Maybe that's what they smuggled out of Afghanistan."

"There are plenty of weapons here. Why would someone go to all the trouble to steal some from Afghanistan? Also, if Carson was involved, why would he tell you he witnessed it?"

"The answer to your first question, is maybe there's a terrorist cell that someone is trying to supply with military grade weapons under the radar. I'm not sure about the answer to your second question. He obviously wouldn't tell me about the weapons he saw being transported if he was somehow involved. Maybe another person on the airplane helped to smuggle them into the US."

"I'll see what I can find out from the base commander and determine if he ever performed an investigation. But first, I want to pursue the woman Carson talked to in the schoolhouse in Afghanistan. Do you think you would recognize her if I could provide you with photos of the females working for the World Aid group?"

"It's unlikely. She was wearing a khimar that covered most of her face, and the room was dark."

"Then that leaves us with capturing Carson and convincing him that we have enough evidence to put him away for a very long time. Then maybe he would be willing to accept a plea deal in exchange for a reduced sentence, if he can provide names of his accomplices and the location of the merchandise that was transported here."

"I know the only evidence you have to any of this is my statement and that's not enough to convict Carson. If he doesn't cooperate, then we are back to square one."

"Carson doesn't know that, though, which is why someone wants you dead."

"So where do we go from here?" Wyatt asked.

"I need to talk to my superiors and let them know what I've discovered so I can proceed with getting a warrant for Carson's arrest and a search warrant to see if we can locate any evidence at his parents' house or their cabin. I also need to determine what, if anything, the CO was able to discover about the weapons Carson witnessed being removed from the airplane and placed in the delivery truck."

"Carson won't be easy to locate. He has his military training, along with being raised as a survivalist on his side. He can hole up in the woods for a very long time."

"Trust me, we have our ways. In the meantime, though, you need to stay somewhere safe."

"I'm tired of hiding. What if you use me as bait to catch whoever is after me? Assign some FBI guys to watch my back. I guarantee it won't be long before they try to kill me again."

"That could be awfully risky. You might get killed, and there goes my only witness."

"You already said that my sole testimony isn't enough to convict him. So what do you have to lose?"

"I'll promise you this. If my superiors agree, then we will try to set up a discreet detail to keep an eye on you. I'll be in contact with Charlie tomorrow and let him know how to proceed. Until then, do not let yourself be seen in public. Agree?"

"Yes."

"It's almost midnight and I have a long drive. Let me discuss with Charlie what little we know and that I plan to contact him tomorrow."

Wyatt and Kate joined the others waiting for them in the family room. Wyatt met Jo's pleading eyes and smiled to let her know he remembered. Kate filled them in on what to expect tomorrow, and Charlie agreed to support whatever she needed.

Kate left to drive back to Virginia. Charlie assured Jo and Wyatt, "You'll be safe here tonight. Keep the blinds drawn in your rooms so no one can see inside. I know we all need some sleep for whatever tomorrow holds. Jo, call your parents to let them know you'll be staying here tonight."

Jo didn't argue. She was too tired. She knew her parents would be waiting up to hear from her, so she didn't hesitate before making the call. She assured them that she was safe and that this would all be over soon.

After Charlie and Carol went to bed, Wyatt and Moose joined Jo in her room. "What do you think you're doing?"

"Shhh. I'll sleep better knowing you are close," Wyatt whispered.

Jo scooted over to make enough room for Wyatt and Moose. She realized that she liked having Wyatt close and never wanted him to leave. "I love you, too," Jo whispered, not sure if Wyatt was still awake to hear.

Chapter 14

The phone rang the next morning while Wyatt and Jo were having breakfast with Carol and Charlie. It was Kate sharing the news that she had arranged a team of FBI agents to perform surveillance to catch whoever was trying to kill Wyatt and Jo. The agents were en route and would be in place by lunch. Jo and Wyatt were told to return to work after noon to try to attract the attention of whoever was after them. The team would be in place to protect them if anyone tried anything. Charlie just needed to get the small town rumor mill going to let everyone know Wyatt had started to work at Burt's garage. That way, hopefully, the person(s) trying to kill him would try again while Wyatt's detail was in place.

Charlie drove Jo, Wyatt, and Moose back to the police station after lunch to pick up Jo's truck. Wyatt and Jo stopped by her house on the way to work just long enough to change clothes. As soon as Jo pulled into the auto parts store parking lot, they noticed a black four door sedan across the street with two men inside.

"That must be the detail assigned to watch you," Wyatt said.

"Yeah, no one will notice them," Jo joked.

"You keep Moose with you again today. I'll pick you both up after work."

Jo leaned over and kissed Wyatt. "Be careful."

"You too. Keep an eye out for anyone suspicious."

Jo got out of the truck with Moose and looked back as Wyatt drove away. She had a sick feeling in the pit of her stomach.

Wyatt proceeded to drive to work, keeping an eye out for anyone that might be following him. He was almost disappointed when he arrived at the garage and no cars had taken any interest in him. He parked the truck off to the side of the parking lot to allow room for the customers to park. He cautiously looked around to make sure no one was waiting to surprise him. His detail was a little more inconspicuous. They were nowhere in sight.

Charlie had informed Burt about Wyatt's predicament so he wouldn't be caught off guard if anyone strange started to hang around. "Hi, Wyatt. Glad you could make it back today." Burt winked at him to show he was on board with the FBI's plan.

"What can I help you with today?" Wyatt asked.

"That car on jacks belongs to the man in the waiting room. It needs the oil changed and tires rotated."

"I'll get right on it." Wyatt decided to introduce himself to the man sitting in the waiting area just in case he was the person assigned to watch him from the FBI. He was wearing blue jeans and a flannel shirt. His attire didn't scream, I'm an FBI agent. "I'll be working on your car today if you have any questions."

"My name is Jason. I'm visiting from out of town and I'm not in any rush. I plan to be here all day."

That answered Wyatt's question. He was from the FBI. "Very good. Glad you could stop by."

The day was nearing the end and Wyatt started to worry the person after him wasn't going to show. He didn't want the FBI to think this was all a waste of their time. He hoped Jason hadn't scared his assailant off. Then a beige Camry pulled into the parking lot.

"Burt, I can help this customer. Why don't you go inside and start closing up?"

Burt looked up as the guy got out of the car. He didn't recognize him. He understood what Wyatt was trying to do. "Sure, holler if you need any help."

Wyatt wiped the grease from his hands and stood beside a five drawer tool cabinet just in case he needed to jump for cover. He let the guy approach him. "What can I help you with today?"

The man smiled as he stepped inside the bay. Then, without flinching, he pulled a gun from his back and started shooting.

Wyatt dove behind the tool cabinet. Jason, who was still sitting in the waiting room, came to life and returned fire.

The shooter fell to the ground. Jason rushed to the fallen man's side and kicked the weapon out of the shooter's hand. Another member of the FBI team appeared within seconds from out of nowhere. Jason stood with his gun trained on the guy, bleeding from the shoulder, on the ground. He yelled to Wyatt, "Are you hit?"

"No!"

"Good! Stay where you are until we get this guy secured."

Wyatt could already hear sirens in the background and knew Charlie must have had his men patrolling close. The ambulance arrived after several police cruisers.

Once the shooter was loaded onto the gurney and strapped in place, Wyatt approached. He stared at the man's face. The man had shaved and trimmed his hair since the last time he had seen him but he recognized him immediately. "You're the man that broke into Jo's house that was supposedly an undercover ATF agent. Where is your partner?"

The shooter didn't say a word. He was loaded into the back of the ambulance and rushed away.

Jason approached Charlie, now on the scene, "The FBI will be standing guard at the hospital 24/7 until the prisoner can be transported to a federal holding facility."

"Understand. Let me know if my men can help in any way."

Wyatt lowered Jason's vehicle from the lift in the garage that he had been pretending to work on all day. "Thanks for catching this guy and stopping him before he could get a clean shot at me. This is the same man that broke into Jo's house a few nights ago. Charlie took him and his partner in for questioning, but had to let them go."

"Hopefully we can get this guy to give up his partner. But until then, stay alert in case he wants to finish what they started."

Charlie spoke up, "I'll share what little information I have on his partner. I'm sure it was probably all fabricated and they have nothing to do with ATF. Jo and you are welcome to stay at my house until we can get this all sorted out."

"I appreciate the offer and everything you have done, but Jo and I'll be fine at her house. I have installed a security system with cameras and motion sensors so no one can sneak up on us. At the first sign of trouble, we'll give you a call."

Charlie wasn't happy with Wyatt's response, but understood. He would have an officer patrol Jo's neighborhood until he was sure everyone involved was caught.

Wyatt's cell phone started to ring and he saw that it was Jo. He answered it, but before he could say a word, Jo spoke up, "I heard the ambulance go through town. Are you all right?"

"Yes. The FBI captured one of the men trying to kill me. There is no need to worry. He's on his way to the hospital after being shot. It was the same man that broke into your house three nights ago that told Charlie he worked for ATF."

"You're kidding, you mean to tell me Charlie had them in custody and they managed to hide their true identities?"

"It appears so."

"I feared it was you in that ambulance."

"Jason, from the FBI, assigned to protect me, didn't give him a chance. He returned fire and hit the suspect before he could get off a clean shot."

"So now what?"

"I feel like celebrating. How about I pick up you and Moose, then stop by the grocery store and buy some steaks, a big bottle of Merlot, and any dessert your heart desires?"

"I have an idea what we can do for dessert," Jo teased.

"Don't be cruel and say that unless you mean it."

"How soon can you get here?"

"I'm on my way!" Wyatt hadn't felt this good in a long time. He finally felt free. He knew Carson and possibly one other guy were still on the loose, but he didn't think they would be bold enough to come after him after today. He drove through downtown Wheeler and approached the one streetlight a block from Jo's Dad's store. The light turned green and he proceeded underneath the streetlight when a car came barreling through the intersection, slamming into his driver's side door with such force it flipped the truck on its' side.

Jo heard the horrible crashing sound of metal from inside the store and took off running. Moose outpaced her, even with his injured hip.

Wyatt lay unconscious in the truck, unaware of the gunman standing in front of the cracked windshield about to shoot him.

Moose, with every ounce of energy he had, leaped into the air and latched on to the right arm of the man holding the gun. Moose crunched down with such force you could hear the bones being crushed. The man immediately dropped the gun and screamed in agony.

Jo grabbed the man's gun and pointed it at his chest. Moose still had a tight hold around the man's arm. "Moose, release!" Jo commanded.

To Jo's surprise, he obeyed. Moose relaxed his grip and sat inches from the man on the ground clutching his arm. The deepest growl Jo had ever heard came from the depth of Moose's soul. "Good boy!" Then in a voice with enough force to stop an army from charging she said, "Don't move or you won't live to see another day!"

Jo's Dad pulled his truck beside the accident scene and took control. "Give me the gun! Go check on Wyatt," he ordered.

Jo handed him the weapon. She kneeled down, looking through the cracked windshield of her truck. She could see Wyatt inside, suspended in mid air, hanging limp from his seat belt. He wasn't moving. She quickly searched for something to help her gain access when she spotted Pete, the cook at Stacy's diner, come rushing up beside her.

"Step out of the way! I'll break through the windshield using this crowbar." He smashed through the glass, then took off his t-shirt and wrapped it around his hand. He peeled back the windshield and carefully slipped inside. He stood on the passenger side door panel and lifted Wyatt, to remove the tension on the seat belt. "Take the knife from my front pocket and cut through the seat belt."

Jo pulled the knife from Pete's pocket. She strained to reach the seat belt and slice through the strap. She stepped out of the way as the strap broke free and Wyatt fell limp into Pete's strong arms. Pete carefully stepped through the windshield opening as the sound of broken glass crunched beneath his worn tennis shoes. He carried Wyatt to the sidewalk and gently laid him on the ground.

Jo felt for a pulse and was relieved to feel a thump. "He's alive!" she screamed. Blood trickled down Wyatt's face and left arm. She tried to stop the bleeding with her hand as the siren from an approaching ambulance could be heard in the distance.

Charlie arrived and handcuffed the man that had rammed his vehicle into Wyatt's. The EMT's prepared Wyatt for transport then loaded him into the back of the ambulance. Moose tried to follow,

154

but Jo wrapped her arms around his neck to stop him. "Sorry boy, you have to stay here with me." That's when she noticed blood streaming down Moose's injured hip.

"Dad, Moose has opened his wound back up, and is bleeding," Jo said as she tried to hold back her emotions.

Her Dad gently lifted Moose into his arms. "Follow me." He carried Moose to his truck parked by the curb.

Jo opened the back door and helped her Dad place Moose gently across the back seat. She climbed in, cradling his head in her lap. "Lay still, boy," she said as she calmly stroked Moose's head.

"I'll take Moose to the vet and stay with him while you take my truck to the hospital. If I need a ride, I'll call you mother. Don't worry honey, I'll make sure the vet takes good care of him."

They arrived at the veterinary hospital and Jo raced inside to find the doctor that had previously treated Moose's injuries. She explained what had happened as Jo's Dad laid Moose on the examination table. She stayed just long enough to make sure that Moose was in good hands. "Thanks for all your help, Dad. Call me when you know how he's doing," Jo said as she rushed out the door.

"And you call me as soon as you know Wyatt's condition," he yelled back.

Jo stomped on the gas pedal, exceeding the speed limit as she raced to the hospital to be with Wyatt. She ran through the emergency room doors and stopped in front of the receptionist's desk. The woman behind the desk was not the same as when Wyatt had been brought in after finding him unconscious by the pond. "Can you tell me where they have taken Wyatt Deckster?"

"What relation are you to the patient?"

Jo thought fast, "My name is Jo McAlester and I'm his fiancé." She stuffed her left hand in her pocket so the receptionist couldn't see there was no engagement ring on her finger.

"He was taken to an exam room through those double doors, but you'll need to stay here." She pointed to the waiting area. "The doctor will come out and speak with you once he has finished his evaluation."

Jo joined a few other weary people sitting waiting for news of their loved ones. Before she could take a seat, Kate, the FBI agent that had interviewed Wyatt, came walking toward her.

"I just heard. Is Wyatt all right?"

"He was unconscious when they loaded him into the ambulance. I haven't been able to get a status on his condition since I arrived."

"Let me see what I can do," Kate said as she disappeared around the corner.

Jo took a seat and glanced down at her hands. They were covered in Wyatt's and Moose's dried blood. She found the restroom and scrubbed the dark red from her hands as she started to shake uncontrollably. Tears ran down her face as she feared the worst. What would she do if Wyatt couldn't recover from his injures this time? She splashed water on her face to wash away the tears. She dried her face with a couple of paper towels and took several deep breaths to try to calm herself. She needed to stay strong and couldn't fall apart yet. "God, I know you brought Wyatt into my life for a reason. Please don't take him yet. Moose and I still need him. Please help him to heal his injuries once again," she prayed out loud. Her eyes welled up with tears again.

Once Jo had her emotions under control, she returned to the emergency room and found Kate waiting for her. "What did you find out?"

"The doctor has the bleeding under control and he's currently doing some x-rays and a CAT Scan to determine the extent of Wyatt's injuries. He has regained consciousness, which is a good sign."

"That is good news. Thank you so much for checking on him for me. Have you had a chance to speak with the guy that tried to shoot Wyatt at Burt's garage?"

"Yes, I just came from his room where they are treating his gunshot wound. He isn't exactly cooperating. Now that we have his partner in custody from the car crash, we can start playing them against each other until one of them breaks their code of silence. They always talk when they think the other is betraying them."

"Hopefully Wyatt will be safe, now that they are both in custody."

"That still leaves Carson on the loose, who might be involved in all this. I'll have an agent stay close to Wyatt while he's in the hospital to make sure no one else tries anything. I have to run, but give me a call if you need anything." Kate handed Jo a card with her cell phone number on it.

Jo found a seat in the corner facing the television. She tried to watch an old rerun of Matlock but was having trouble focusing. She stood up and started to pace. An hour passed and there was still no word on Wyatt's condition. Then her cell phone rang. It was her Dad. "How's Moose?"

"The vet said it didn't appear as if there was any additional damage to the hip. He closed the wound with more stitches and wrapped his leg back to the splint to restrict his movement. German Shepherd's have a high threshold for pain, and he didn't want Moose performing any more heroic acts until his hip had a chance to heal. I'm going to bring him home with me. How's Wyatt?"

"All I've heard is that the bleeding is under control and that he regained consciousness. I'm still waiting to hear from the doctor. He was taken for a CAT Scan and x-rays about an hour ago."

"Call me when you hear something."

"Will do. Hug Moose for me."

As Jo ended the call she heard her name being called. "I'm Jo," she spoke up.

"Why don't we have a seat over here and I can go over Wyatt's condition with you?"

That didn't sound good, Jo thought. She took a chair next to the doctor.

"Let me start by telling you I think Wyatt should make a full recovery."

Jo breathed a sigh of relief.

"That being said, though, he sustained some pretty serious injuries. The x-rays show he broke his collarbone and several ribs. His left arm will have to remain in a sling for a while. The CAT Scan showed a little brain swelling, but no brain bleeds were evident. He has a severe concussion. He has some bruising on

157

his left hip, but it isn't broken. Knowing this is not his first head injury, I would like to keep him here overnight for observation. If there are no complications, I should be able to release him tomorrow."

"Thank you so much, doctor. Can I see him?"

"I have to warn you, he's a little out of it with pain meds right now. Follow me and I'll show you to the examination room where he's resting. Arrangements are being made to move him to a private room shortly."

Jo followed the doctor through the double swinging doors. She walked down the brightly lit hall, past a few rooms before turning to the left. "You can sit in here with him while you wait for him to be moved to a room," the doctor said.

Jo entered quietly so as not to disturb Wyatt. He lay with his eyes closed. There were stitches across his forehead to stop the bleeding. His face was bruised and swollen and his left arm was in a sling.

Wyatt cracked his swollen eyes open and managed a slight smile at Jo. He used his free right arm to reach for her hand. He spoke softly, "The nurse told me my fiancé was waiting to see me."

"I was afraid since I wasn't family they wouldn't give me your status, and that's all I could come up with in a split second."

"I kind of like the sound of that."

"I think your head injury may have messed with your brain," Jo said, trying to be funny. Then she realized how harsh that sounded. "You know I love you and can't wait to spend more time with you after all this is over."

"That's if you survive putting up with me while I heal from my injuries. You know I don't make a very good patient."

Jo leaned down and kissed Wyatt passionately on the lips. "I might be able to make your stay in bed more entertaining," she joked.

Wyatt kissed back, enjoying her mouth against his. Their kiss was interrupted by two of the hospital staff wheeling in a gurney.

"We're here to take you to your room, Mr. Deckster. Let us do all the work moving you from the bed to the gurney. Understand?"

"Yes," Wyatt said.

They lowered his bed so it was at the same level as the gurney and gently slid him over.

Jo followed as they wheeled Wyatt down the hall and into the elevator. They rode up one floor before getting off. They pushed him in a room right across from the nurses station. Jason, the FBI agent that had saved Wyatt from being shot, was already in place, waiting for them to arrive.

"I save you from getting shot and this is how you repay me," Jason joked.

"Believe me, it wasn't by choice. Jo, I would like for you to meet Jason, with the FBI. He was assigned to keep an eye on me today."

"Thanks for capturing his shooter. Kate told me someone would be staying close to Wyatt while he was in the hospital. Is that going to be you?"

"Yes, I volunteered for guard duty until Kate can get someone here to relieve me. I'll stay outside your room by the nurses' station and will make sure you're not disturbed."

"Thanks," Wyatt said. Once they were alone he realized Moose wasn't with Jo. "The hospital wouldn't let you bring in Moose this time?"

Jo got emotional at remembering how Moose risked everything to stop the guy from shooting Wyatt through the truck windshield. Tears came to her eyes.

"Did something happen to Moose?" Wyatt asked anxiously.

"He'll be fine," Jo blurted out, to calm Wyatt's fears. "You should be so proud of him. He saved your life today. When I heard the collision I came running, but Moose beat me to the scene. The man that crashed into you was about to shoot you through the windshield. Moose grabbed hold of the man's right arm, causing him to drop his gun. He bit down with such force you could hear the man's bones being crushed. Once I recovered the man's gun and pointed it at him, I yelled for Moose to release. You know what, he actually listened to my command. He released the man's arm and sat staring menacingly at him until Charlie arrived and took control."

"But that doesn't explain why he's not here with you. Did he get hurt?"

"The wound on his hip opened back up. My Dad took us to the vet and stayed with him while I came here to check on you. The vet sutured his hip back up to stop the bleeding and secured the splint on his leg to limit his movement. My Dad is taking him home with him tonight and will watch him for us until you're released."

"Does that mean you're going to stay here with me tonight?"

"You're stuck with me," Jo said as she kissed Wyatt gently on the lips.

Chapter 15

The next morning Jo downed a large cup of coffee while Wyatt tried to stomach the powdered eggs and dry toast he was given for breakfast. Kate suddenly appeared at his door.

"I have some news," Kate announced.

"Were you able to get one of the guys to talk?" Jo asked eagerly.

"As a matter of fact I did, and was quite surprised by what he revealed. The merchandise that was taken from the Taliban the day you were injured was the family of one of its leaders, his three wives and twelve children."

"So what does that have to do with me?" Wyatt asked.

"This leader is trying to make a statement by killing anyone that might be involved. I think the women went willingly to escape from their abusive husband. Rachel, the woman you saw in the schoolhouse who worked for the World Aid group, must've met these wives while providing aid to their village. Once she saw the injuries these wives had sustained at the hand of their husband, she couldn't stand by and do nothing. She arranged for transport to the US to protect them from any additional harm. She couldn't go through normal channels, though, for fear the husband would find out and kill them for betraying him. The men that have been trying to kill you are mercenaries hired by their husband. The husband is trying to save face, have his family returned to him, and the people responsible killed. Rachel was found brutally murdered with her head chopped off, shortly after the merchandise went missing, so to speak. I have to assume she is the one that got the wives out of the country, which is why she was killed and put on public display. The husband wanted to show how powerful he was and that he would not stand for anyone disrespecting him."

"Do you think Rachel broke under pressure during interrogation and shared who helped take his family?" Jo asked.

"It's possible she gave them Carson's name and the Taliban figured out the rest on their own. We still don't know what happened to the women and children once they arrived in this country. We're trying to track down the names of the airplane pilots and those who helped offload the cargo once it arrived back in the United States. We have no idea where the women may be today."

Jo spoke up, "I have an idea where they might be hiding out."

Wyatt looked over at Jo. "How could you possibly know?"

"When you were talking with Carson in the family room, I was in the kitchen. There was way more food in the refrigerator than one person could possibly eat. Plus, the pantry was stocked with food you would find in a house with children; Lucky Charms cereal, Oreo's, and animal crackers. Does that sound like food Carson would eat?"

"No, but we were in the house for several hours and saw no signs of anyone else."

"Maybe he had them stashed somewhere else or hidden in another room. I just know they were probably someplace close when we were there," Jo added.

"That would explain why Carson is AWOL. He knew if he returned to Afghanistan he would end up dead like the woman that worked for the World Aid group. I still don't understand why he didn't tell me what was really going on."

"He was probably just trying to protect you from the truth. The less you knew, the better off he figured you would be," Jo said.

"So, who are the guys that were disguised as ATF agents who broke into Jo's house?" Wyatt asked.

"The man that tried to shoot you at Burt's garage and the man that ran into your truck had fake ATF credentials on them. That's how they were able to convince local authorities that they were undercover ATF agents. In reality, they were trying to kill you to receive the one hundred thousand bounty that the Taliban leader put on your and Carson's heads. One of the men also confessed to being the one that lured you to Old Mill Pond Road. He wore a disguise, which is why you didn't recognize him as one of the men that broke into Jo's."

"But what about the ATF agents that tried to enter Carson's cabin in Idaho? They didn't look fake," Wyatt asked.

"I also have been doing some checking into that," Kate said. "I was able to contact the Commanding Officer that Carson talked to at the base in Texas regarding the weapons he witnessed being offloaded onto the panel truck. The commander did take his account seriously and found security footage showing the delivery truck picking up the crate of weapons."

"Was he able to locate the weapons?" Wyatt asked.

"Unfortunately, the delivery truck was found abandoned and empty in a vacant lot just down the road from the base. He lost track of the weapons after that. He did alert base security to watch for any late night deliveries and to stop all vehicles to search for any unauthorized cargo inside before allowing them to leave the base."

"Did they find any more weapons being transported?" Jo asked.

"About two months ago, a delivery truck was stopped and searched at the gate. Guess what they found inside? A crate full of weapons. The men driving the truck were taken into custody. They were on homeland's watch list and suspected of being tied to a terrorist organization located here in the states. The problem remains, though, that there is someone in Afghanistan who is helping to smuggle these weapons out of the country. None of the people arrested have shared who that might be. It could be they just don't know."

"That still doesn't explain why ATF is looking into Carson."

"The CO decided to check out everyone in your unit to see if there was a connection. Of the eight men, five remain in service and have returned to Afghanistan. Carson was listed as a person of interest because he's AWOL and traveled home on the same airplane as the weapons."

"Why would Carson tell the CO about the weapons if he was the one that helped smuggle them?" Wyatt asked.

"Maybe so he wouldn't be suspected."

"So where does that leave us?" Wyatt asked.

"ATF is actively working to isolate how the weapons are being smuggled here and are still trying to locate Carson. If we can find

163

Carson first, we might be able to discover where the women and children he helped smuggle into the US are staying. Then we can talk to the women and hopefully get them to provide information as to where their husband, the Taliban leader, may be hiding."

"What about the men that have been trying to kill me? They don't know where their boss is located?"

"The men we have in custody won't give us a name or how they contact him. I'm hoping it's only a matter of time before one of the men will want to negotiate for a better deal and provide us with that information, but we don't have the luxury of time on our side. We need to find Carson before ATF does."

"You know getting Carson to turn himself in and share where the Taliban leaders family is hidden is unlikely," Wyatt said.

"You seem to have a connection with Carson. Do you think you could get him to meet you someplace so we could ask him some questions about the women and children?"

"No, he wouldn't be that stupid. He would know something is up right away, especially since Jo and I took off without saying good-bye the last time we saw him."

"If we could just speak with the women he helped smuggle out of Afghanistan, we could offer them immunity and asylum in exchange for them providing information on the possible whereabouts of their husband. We could also offer them protection. Carson won't be able to keep them hidden forever. It's just a matter of time before their husband's hired killers find them."

"I have an idea, if you're up for a road trip," Wyatt said. "What if you and I go to Idaho and visit with Carson's parents? They were very helpful the last time I was there, providing me with Carson's location. I could try to explain to them what Carson has gotten himself mixed up in and how dangerous it has become. Carson's parents may be able to persuade him to meet with us."

Jo had sat by quietly listening for a while, but could no longer hold her tongue. "You are in no condition to travel!"

"I can rest in the back seat of a car as well as I can in this bed. When Carson's parents get a look at me they will want to protect their son from experiencing the same fate, or worse. I'm the best chance we have of finding Carson and the wives before their husband does."

"I don't like it, but I know you're probably right. But if you think you're going without me, you're mistaken. We have gotten this far together and I don't plan on letting you go alone."

Wyatt smiled at Jo's tenacity and reached for her hand. "I wouldn't think of leaving you behind."

***

Kate made the necessary arrangements to fly them to Boise, Idaho. Wyatt was released from the hospital with a bottle of pain pills gripped tightly in his right hand. He soon discovered that the slightest movement made him gasp from the pain from his broken ribs. He quickly learned to take short breaths. A wheelchair transported Wyatt to the airplane to limit his activity.

Jo stayed by Wyatt's side to try to make him as comfortable as possible during their journey. She worried that the change in pressure might bring on a headache from the concussion. Thankfully, the flight was smooth and the effects of the pain pills helped Wyatt to doze.

Kate rented an SUV upon arrival in Idaho to take them the rest of the way to the ranch owned by Carson's parents. So far everything was going as planned. They arrived at Carson's parents ranch by mid-afternoon. This time the heavy, wooden gate was locked securely.

"Now what do we do?" Jo asked.

"This may actually be a good sign. You said the gate was closed but unlocked the last time you were here. Maybe Carson is hiding at home with the wives and children and they have increased security to protect them. Look, there on top of the gate post. There's a camera. Maybe if we get out of the car so they can see us, someone will come and let us in."

"At this point we've got nothing to lose," Wyatt said.

Jo reached out her arm and helped Wyatt climb from the back seat of the SUV. He placed his right arm around Jo's neck and slowly walked around the vehicle until he was standing in front of the camera. Kate stepped out of the driver's seat, stood in front of the camera, and held up her FBI credential. To their delight, they saw a truck approach from the other side of the gate.

Dale Marshall stepped out of the truck. "What can I help you with today?"

Wyatt spoke up. "Remember me? I met you a few days ago when I stopped by looking for Carson. You were very helpful and I got a chance to speak with him. As you can see, I've had an accident since then. The same people that did this to me are also after Carson. Kate is with the FBI and wants to make sure your son and the people he is protecting are safe."

"I think you will want to hear what I have to say. If you would just open the gate and give me a chance to explain, I promise no harm will come to you or your son," Kate said.

Dale Marshall hesitated, then did what his heart knew was best; he opened the gate.

Kate followed the truck down the lane and stopped when she reached the front of the house. Dale showed them inside.

"Dad, what have you done!"

"Carson, you can't continue to hide forever. Now let's just all sit down in the den and hear what they have to say."

Wyatt spoke up. "Carson, you have to trust me. I'm trying to help."

Carson looked at Wyatt and realized he was injured. "What happened?"

"Two men tried to kill me, but the FBI managed to stop them before they succeeded. You need to listen to what she has to say."

They all moved to the den. Ellen, Carson's Mom, brought in a tray with a large coffee carafe, pitcher of creamer, bowl of sugar, and several mugs; sensing they could use the warmth and the caffeine.

"Before I start, I just want to thank you for letting us into your home. Carson, what I have to share is quite graphic. Are you comfortable with having your parents here?" Kate asked.

"Yes, I have nothing to hide from them."

"To begin with, the two men that tried to kill Wyatt were hired by the husband of the women you helped escape from Afghanistan." Kate stopped to get Carson's reaction.

"But Wyatt didn't have anything to do with that."

"I know, but Wyatt was in the schoolhouse with you that day and must have been seen. It wasn't until recently that Wyatt's location was discovered, which is when all the trouble started for him. The husband is desperate to show his men that he's still in control and will stop at nothing to bring his family back."

"They are hidden somewhere safe where he'll never find them," Carson said.

"That may be true for the time being, but you know they can't hide for the rest of their lives. The only way they will ever truly be free is to provide us with information to where their husband can be found. If they can give me the location of the different Taliban compounds where he might be located, then we can stop him from doing any more harm. Even though it has been almost a year since they were in Afghanistan, they should be able to provide valuable intel as to the possible whereabouts of their husband. I can ensure them asylum and provide them with new identities, if needed. You obviously cared for Rachel, who worked for the World Aid group, which is why you offered to help get the women and children out of the country. I'm sure you heard what happened to Rachel after you met at the schoolhouse. Don't let the same thing happen to these brave women and children. They deserve a chance for a normal life."

"I know someone within the ATF is involved with trying to hunt me down. How do you know others in the government aren't involved?"

"ATF is trying to track you down because you came forward about the weapons you saw being offloaded at the base. They captured one man trying to leave with another shipment of weapons, but haven't been able to track down who the other players are that are involved. Since you're AWOL, they thought you might be able to help identify other suspects. But that's not my concern. I just want to talk to the women and see if they can provide information on their husband. I don't necessarily have to meet with the women face to face. I can set up a secure video conference with them so no one can discover their location. That way they can share what they know without having to reveal where they're staying."

Carson thought about that for a few seconds. He sadly looked at Wyatt and focused on his injures. He noticed the sling wrapped around his neck supporting his injured collar bone and the tired, dark circles under his eyes. He felt like Wyatt looked, tired to the core, doing everything in his power to keep the women and children safe. "You have to believe me when I say I never meant for you to be involved in any of this. I thought if I blew up the school it would provide the distraction for our unit to get away and conceal what really occurred that day. I know I didn't share with you everything that had happened. I was just testing you to see what you actually remembered."

"So what really happened that day?" Wyatt asked.

Carson spoke, looking directly at Wyatt. "I left out the part about the dead bodies of some women and children, that had been killed earlier in the day, being placed in the schoolhouse to help conceal what we truly had planned. Their village had been raided by the Taliban. Rachel, my friend with the World Aid group, got the idea that if their burned bodies were discovered inside the rubble of the schoolhouse, that just maybe we could fool the husband into believing they were the bodies of his wives and children that we helped escape. I didn't anticipate you and Rob following me over to the school. The two men that jumped you were trying to protect Rachel and didn't realize you meant her no harm. Rob being shot was just a terrible accident. I told our commander that I investigated the schoolhouse on my own and discovered weapons were being stored inside, which you now know to be a lie. I also told him that I saw you being attacked and tried to help, but by the time I arrived Rob had been shot and the men ran away. I explained to the commander that I blew up the schoolhouse so the weapons couldn't be used against us. But the news media had a field day and said US soldiers bombed a schoolhouse filled with women and children. We just wanted the husband of the wives we smuggled to believe his family had been killed in the school, but never meant for our unit to take the blame. Our plan to conceal the escape of women and children worked, that is until Rachel was captured and tortured. After she was killed, everything started to fall apart. I couldn't return to our unit and risk the lives of the other US service personnel."

"What happened once the women and children landed in the US?" Kate asked.

"A friend of Rachel's worked on the ground crew at the Fort Lauderdale airport and was responsible for offloading the pallets of cargo from the World Air cargo airplane. He was told there would be a crate with some precious cargo and to handle it with care. When the airplane landed just after midnight, he was to move the crate to a waiting truck without customs seeing him. The truck was to drive a few miles down the road to a truck stop. An organization that helps women leave abusive relationships was to be waiting for them to arrive. The women and children were to be transferred to a large van and taken someplace where they wouldn't be found. But then the people involved with the move started showing up dead. First, it was Rachel, then it was the two men that attacked you at the schoolhouse, then it was Rachel's friend that worked on the ground crew at the Fort Lauderdale airport. The woman who drove the van to the truck stop was one of the few remaining people who knew their location. She became scared she would be killed next. Rachel had given her my number and told her to call me if she ran into any trouble. She contacted me a few weeks after I arrived home, begging for my help. That's when I secretly moved them to my parents' cabin. But then, after it was raided, I knew our location had been compromised."

"But we were in the cabin for a few hours and didn't see or hear them," Wyatt said.

"They were hiding in the attic. I moved them there when I heard you at the door. After you left, I made sure no one followed you down the logging road. Then I loaded everyone in my suburban and we escaped down the same logging road. I drove by the tavern and saw you and Jo sitting in the van. I decided the less you knew the better, and kept driving."

"Jo and I decided we couldn't trust you, and drove away before we thought you saw us," Wyatt added.

"Now that we all know what happened, can we proceed with making arrangements to speak with the women?" Kate asked.

"I still don't trust that you'll be able to protect them if I turn them over. I would feel better if the women talked with whoever you need them to through a secure video conference line until their husband is captured. You provide me with the number to call and the time and I'll set it up at my end," Carson said.

"That sounds reasonable. It'll take me a day to gather up the necessary personnel at my end. How do you want me to contact you with the information?"

"You can contact my parents and they will get me the information."

"Do you want me to assign some security personnel to watch your parents' house to keep them safe until all this is over?"

Dale spoke up, "That won't be necessary. No one can approach this ranch without being seen. If anyone tries to breach my property, they will be very sorry."

"Before we leave, are there any questions?"

"No, I'll wait to hear from you. Wyatt and Jo, you are welcome to stay here with my parents until all this is over."

Wyatt looked into Jo's eyes, searching for what she wanted him to do.

Jo spoke up, "He's your brother. I think we can trust him."

"If it wouldn't be too much trouble for your parents, I appreciate the offer. I don't want to put Jo's family in any more danger."

"It's no trouble at all. Carson, why don't you show them to the guest rooms? Kate, would you like to stay for supper before you head out?" Ellen asked.

"No. I'm afraid I don't have time. I need to get back to Virginia and set everything in motion for our meeting tomorrow. Thanks once again for your hospitality and welcoming us into your lovely home," Kate said, picking up her leather attaché case and heading for the door.

Carson stayed just long enough to eat supper. "I must leave to make arrangements with the women for their upcoming meeting. My parents will take good care of you while I'm gone. I'll contact you once I determine it's safe. Hopefully, all this will be over soon. I look forward to being able to spend some time with you and get to know the brother I never knew I had."

***

Wyatt stood on Dale and Ellen's back patio looking out over the pasture behind their house. Enjoying the peace and quiet that surrounded him, he hoped that one day he and Jo could own a

170

farm. He dared to imagine having a few horses, cows, and maybe a few hens to lay fresh eggs every day. It had been three days since Carson and the women had met with the FBI. He hadn't heard anything from Kate or Carson since the day he had arrived. He was starting to think the worst. Had their location been compromised?

"Wyatt, come here!" Jo yelled from inside the house.

"What is it?"

"Look!" Jo pointed at the television.

"A Taliban compound was raided last night, killing a prominent leader, along with several members of his security team. This marks a significant effort in the dismantling of the Taliban forces."

"Did you hear that, it's over!" Jo yelled as she gently hugged Wyatt, careful not to put pressure on his injured collarbone or ribs.

"Carson did it. He got the women to tell the FBI where their husband could be found," Wyatt excitedly told Dale and Ellen. They joined in with hugs and cheers. Tears of joy started to flow as the telephone rang.

Dale answered the phone. "It's Kate," he told everyone.

"Did you hear?" Kate asked.

"Yes! I take it the leader killed was the one we were after?"

"Yes. The women no longer have anyone to fear. Will you let Carson know?"

"Yes, I was just about to contact him." Dale hung up the phone and dialed the number Carson had given him to call. All he said was, "It's over. You can come home, son."

Carson must not have been hiding too far away, and showed up an hour later with a carload of women and children. They were happily greeted by the women who spoke broken English. Carson had been teaching them words in English they would need to survive in America, during the past several months while protecting them. The children were dressed in American clothes, but the women still hid their faces with their khimar. They were all welcomed with open arms.

Chapter 16

A few weeks later the news reported a raid on a warehouse full of weapons in Maryland. It was reported that Homeland, along with ATF, had stopped a smuggling ring connected with a terrorist cell. They had fouled their plans for a major attack on US soil.

Carson was charged with desertion, but after explaining the circumstances in front of a military court, he was exonerated of all charges. He was granted an honorable discharge. He moved back to Idaho to help his family with their ranch, and so he could stay close to the women and children he had helped rescue.

Dale and Ellen helped the three women and their children find a place to live not far from them in the surrounding community. Carson visited them frequently, continuing to help them get accustomed to their new way of life. He watched over the women like a big brother and acted as an uncle to the children. Each woman found a job that suited them. One used her knowledge of hand sewing clothes and is now performing alterations in a department store. Another woman's love for baking was put to good use making fresh bread each morning in a local bakery. And the third found her loving ability to care for children useful and opened a day care center for some of the single mothers in their new community.

Jo and Wyatt returned home to many loving kisses from Moose. Wyatt knew he never wanted to be separated from Jo. A few days after returning from Idaho, he asked Jo's parents for their permission to marry their daughter. He was happily given their blessings. The next day he made arrangements for the ring to be hidden in a piece of chocolate overload cake served at Stacy's diner. When they arrived at the diner to eat, Wyatt worried his surprise was going to be spoiled. Almost the entire town showed up to witness the proposal. They sat in the only vacant booth at the back of the restaurant. They ordered a couple of Stacy's famous burgers and fries. When the food was brought to their table, Wyatt could barely eat. His stomach was in knots, worried about what he had planned for dessert. Stacy brought the delicious looking cake, with the ring hidden inside, to their table. She told Jo it was on the house to celebrate her return to town and the role she had played in bringing down the terrorists. Jo smiled with delight at the luscious looking cake and immediately took a big bite. She almost swallowed the ring before Wyatt could stop her. He got down on one knee and proposed as he slid the now chocolate covered diamond ring on her finger. With a mouth still full of cake, Jo said yes, to the delight of the entire diner. She gave him a seductive kiss, smearing his mouth with chocolate.

The entire town came to their wedding just two weeks later. Jo's Dad belonged to the Masonic lodge, which was the perfect location for the reception. A local band played country music and everyone danced the night away on the large dance floor. The sound of joyful music could be heard for blocks. The women in the town loaded the buffet tables with every kind of casserole and sweets you could imagine. Wyatt couldn't afford an expensive honeymoon, so they spent the weekend in Jo's parents' RV. They returned to the beautiful, secluded spot along the small lake in the mountains. It was almost deserted during the winter months and they enjoyed having the place to themselves, cuddling all night to keep each other warm.

Wyatt continued working at Burt's garage and slowly paid off a used truck that Burt had loaned him. He worked full time now, helping to repair the cars of the good people of Wheeler.

Jo still helped her Dad by delivering automobile parts throughout the town, with Moose by her side to keep her company. Her favorite delivery, of course, was to Burt's garage where she got to exchange a kiss for parts from her husband.

Wyatt's dream of owning a farm became a reality when a for sale sign appeared on the lot next door to Jo's house. They were elated when their offer was accepted. They were able to secure a loan through the bank to pay for the property and it closed a month later. Wyatt bought one bull and nine Black Angus to start his herd. A few weeks later, he built a chicken coop for the three hens he picked up at the local farm store. They set aside a small plot of land for a garden, which they planted in the spring.

Moose's hip healed and he enjoyed having the full run of the farm. He kept track of the cows and watched over a stray kitten that appeared one day.

Jo slowly learned how to cook, experimenting with a new concoction each night. Wyatt never complained, no matter how bad the taste. He realized how lucky he was that Jo was the one to find him unconscious by the pond.

Jo found her protector and soulmate where she least expected it, through the eyes of his beloved German Shepherd.

About The Author

Diane E. Izzard is the author of Too Soon To Die, Path To Finding Happiness, Wildflowers By The River, Flying Into Darkness, and Abandoned But Not Lost. She has found her passion in writing cozy mysteries and inspirational novels. She had been writing for five years and her real life feeling stories draw you in and keep you hooked until the very end. She loves dogs, hiking, biking, skiing, and curling up with a good book. Her latest dog, an Alaskan Malamute, provides the personality for the dogs in some of her stories. You can contact her at diane.izzard@yahoo.com.